FAE HUNTED

BOOK THREE IN THE FAE BLOODLINES SERIES

ROSE GARCIA

For Emily P

Meeting you was one of the best Christmas gifts ever!

THE FAE REALM OF

FAEVENLY

TORCH
LAKE

STRONG
HAVEN EAST

SUMMIT
RANGE

GREEN
FALLS

MOTHERS
RIVERS

SAND
LUFF

THE
GREAT
COVE

THE MORNING SEA

PROLOGUE

Julio

T he thing about leaving the fae realm is that you never really leave it.

Celyse and I now lived in the human realm, and had a daughter, but the perils that faced us in Faevenly all those years ago followed us to Texas.

It began with dreams of Draven, the sinister fae vampire witch we thought we had left behind, imprisoned in the dungeon of Strong Haven Palace and held in a deep, magical spell.

He visited my sleep nightly, telling me he'd find us, threatening to obliterate us all. It didn't feel like a dream anymore—it felt like a warning.

His presence stretched into my waking hours, sending tingles at the back of my neck that signaled danger. As if the barrier between us was thinning. I didn't even know if what was happening was real or in my head. So I kept the nightmares to myself, not wanting to worry Celyse. But eventually our little Gabriela started having the same terrifying dreams. Whatever had found me, had found her too. She called them dark nightmares, describing the monster as a tall figure with crystal eyes in a black cloak.

Draven…

I shared with Celyse the horrors of what was happening when I went to bed at night. That's when Gabriela's training began. We taught her how to shoot a bow and arrow, how to wield a sword and a dagger, and how to handle hand-to-hand combat. We even fashioned the strength stone, the aquoise, into a necklace for her to wear. With the power of the stone on her, next to her cross, we hoped it would provide her some sort of protection.

As she grew, so did her fae skills, along with her Avila witchy skills. She started seeing spirits at an early age, and soon after began developing the tingle behind her neck like me. We never really knew how much power she possessed, or what her true gifts were, until one day at the bakery.

That was the day everything changed for us.

The store was short-staffed, so Celyse and I stayed late to close for the evening. Gabriela was with us. She was sitting in the office, working on homework, when three fae entered the bakery.

"Sorry, but we are closing now," Celyse said as she made her way to lock the front door. "You will have to come back another time."

"We only came to see if the daughter of Strong Haven really owned this store. We had heard rumors, but were not sure," answered the tallest of the three.

His long dark hair was pulled back in a ponytail, and he wore a baseball cap. He wasn't the typical slender fae build, but more on the stocky side. As if he had lived in the human realm for a while. There were several fae living here in secret, though we hadn't come across any before that day.

"We don't want any trouble," I warned from behind the counter.

"Trouble? Why would we give you any trouble?" he asked, moving further into the bakery with an aggressive stride, the other two flanking him.

Celyse backed away from the trio, but kept her chin raised and hands fisted at her sides. "You need to leave. Now."

Ignoring her request, he moved in closer. "We would rather stay and talk about your history with Draven. We have long admired his works in Faevenly." His smile turned into a sneer. "You might even call us fans."

I jumped over the counter and planted myself next to Celyse, ready for anything, when Gabriela came out of the office.

"Mom, Dad. What's going on?"

"Thunderation," the intruder gawked, his mouth hanging open. "They have a child."

He charged for Gabriela. Celyse spun and grabbed his arm while the other two fae jumped me. I leveled one with an elbow jab to the throat, but not before a blow crashed into my face and a kick pummeled my gut.

A piercing scream erupted.

At first, I didn't know what it was. The deafening shrill sounded otherworldly. My eyes darted around looking for the source until it landed on Gabriela, mouth open, hand clutching her necklace. A purple blast of light erupted from her, swathing the room in crackles of energy.

The fae that attacked us were obliterated on the spot, turned into particles of dust. And Gabriela immediately passed out. When she came to, it was as if her mind protected her from what she had done, because she didn't remember anything. And Celyse and I didn't tell her.

To safeguard Gabriela and ourselves, we stopped visiting Faevenly. We pushed away that part of our lives because we thought distancing ourselves from it would insulate us from the dangers of the realm.

We no longer talked about shimmers, or the fae, or any other magical creatures. We had all traces of Faevenly removed from our home. We even hid the aquoise stone somewhere where no one would ever find it. We prayed our efforts would keep us from harm.

But sometimes prayers go unanswered.

CHAPTER 1
Gabriela

A cold tingle dashed across the back of my neck as I approached my house. The sensation couldn't be blamed on the weather. It was only the first week of October, and Austin, Texas, was still clinging to its summer heat despite the shifting season.

Slowing the car, I rolled to a stop and cut the engine. I stepped out. I scanned my surroundings the way my mom and dad had taught me when I was little, because something was definitely wrong. Like I wasn't alone. A chill crept down my spine, sharp and sudden, as if something unseen had just turned its attention on me.

My pulse skipped, and that old warning from my childhood whispered through me.

Find the source.

I was only ten when Mom first said those words to me, and I remembered her lesson as if it were yesterday. We were in the backyard tending the garden when the strange feeling overcame me for the first time. I looked up at her with fear in my throat, not understanding why I was suddenly so scared.

"What is it, Gabriela?" she asked, looking down at me with bright green eyes.

With the sunlight behind her, her long blond hair sparkled, the dark streak gleaming like a silky ribbon. I had always wanted to be just like her when I grew up —beautiful, strong, and wise. But more than anything, I wanted to be as brave as her. She wasn't afraid of anything.

Instead, I was her opposite. I wasn't tall and statuesque, but petite and small. I also didn't have light-colored hair with a dark streak, but dark hair with light streaks. And instead of ivory skin and bright green eyes, I had tan skin and brown eyes like my dad. Though sometimes, depending on what I wore, a bit of green could be seen when you looked closely.

I inherited many things from my dad, including the abilities to sense impending danger and to see spirits —abilities I didn't discover until that day in our backyard when I had felt something.

"I-I-I don't know what it is, Momma."

She crouched beside me and stroked my cheek. "When your inner self issues a warning, you must be still. And when you are in control of your mind and your thoughts, you must look. Find the source."

"Look for what?" I asked in a hushed tone, not understanding what she was telling me.

"For whatever is calling to you," she said.

She squeezed my hand as I glanced up at the tall pine trees. The autumn leaves rustled in the wind. Beyond the trees, puffy white clouds trailed their way across the bright blue sky. The unease inside of me started to lessen, and we continued walking into the woods.

Taking slow and careful steps, I hadn't gone too far when I detected movement. A man came into view. He looked soggy and waterlogged with gray-tinged skin and stringy wet hair, as if he had stepped out of the lake waters after having been submerged for a long while. I knew in an instant he was the reason why I was tingly and I buried my face in my hands.

He was my first encounter with a spirit.

The next time I saw *un muerto* was only a few months later, when Dad and I were at the grocery store. We had finished shopping and were pushing our cart through the parking lot to our car when a woman walked by. A gash ripped across her forehead, and dark blood stained her pink shirt.

Dad calmly wrapped his arms around me and held me close. "She's only walking by, Gabriela. Okay? There's nothing to be afraid of, *mija*."

My eyes flicked from my dad to the woman as she meandered her way around the parked cars, looking lost. "What is she doing, Daddy?"

"She's looking for a place where she can cross over to heaven. And I promise you, she will find it."

"She will?" I asked, the idea of the lady going to heaven making me feel better.

"Yes." He smiled, squeezing my hand. "She will."

As the years went by, I forced myself to be brave. Now, at eighteen, bad vibes and dead people didn't faze me. And mostly, I barely even noticed the dead. They had blended into the ordinary fabric of my life, like a tree in a yard, or a car parked on the street.

Oak tree, pine tree, red car, blue truck, dead person.

No big deal.

But why would a spirit be inside my house? Then a different notion altogether dawned on me. What if the tingling I was feeling wasn't a spirit, but a burglar? Whatever it was, I could handle it. I wasn't ten anymore, and I refused to be afraid.

I blew out a breath and straightened my back. "Okay, look, Gabriela. Find the source," I muttered to myself, my mind zipping back to my mom's lesson.

My eyes roamed my sand-colored brick-and-stone home with green trim. The house sat high on a hill, looking down on Lake Travis. Trees nearly shrouded it from view, as if tucking it away and hiding it from the world, the way my parents liked. Our lot was huge, and there were no other houses around. Colorful bushes and flowers of all different shapes and sizes outlined the perimeter. From the paved sidewalk, everything looked as it should.

Then I spotted it.

Leaves usually sprinkled the walkway to the front door this time of year. But today was different. The orange and yellow foliage blanketed the grass, but as I narrowed my stare, I noticed patches missing along the walkway to the door. Had a delivery person kicked the leaves about? Did Mom or Dad come home from the bakery to get something? There were no packages at the door, and the mail had been delivered hours ago. Plus, Mom and Dad rarely came home early from work.

I repositioned my backpack, making sure it was snug against my body, then stepped forward. I could shoot a bow and arrow almost as precisely as my mom, I could handle hand-to-hand combat well enough, and my sword-wielding skills were pretty impressive—so much so I had joined the school fencing team and was their best athlete. But I had never used any of my skills in real life. As in, against a true threat. Honestly, I kind of hoped someone had broken into my house so I could put my skills to the test.

"All right, whoever you are," I whispered to myself, "you've messed with the wrong-ass house."

I slipped the key in the lock and turned. With a soft touch, I eased the door open, then slowly closed it behind me. Slipping my backpack off, I cradled it to the wood floor, then studied the area as my fingers reached for the walking stick kept by the front door. Meeting the smooth wood, my fingers slid around it and held it tight, every muscle in my body tensed.

Silence blanketed the two-story house. The books and papers in the study to the right of the foyer were tidied and in place. Piles of clothes and shoes dotted the stairs as usual, reminding me that I needed to put my stuff away. With not a sound to be heard, and the sensation going away, I relaxed my stance and set the stick back in its place. I had no idea what I had felt, but everything in the house appeared okay.

I kicked off my black boots and was starting through the house when a shadow at the entryway into the kitchen halted me. I spun and lunged for the stick. Grabbing it, I swung back around—and froze. Before me stood someone with long silver hair, pointed ears, and violet eyes, dressed in dark brown and a black cloak.

A fae.

"You." I swallowed with surprise.

"Yes, me." He narrowed his eyes, then slid his own fighting stick from a holster slung across his back. "Are you ready to die today?"

"No," I shot back, getting into a fighting stance with my left leg forward and my right leg back. "Are you?"

He smiled, then answered with a charge. I sidestepped, choking up on my weapon like a baseball bat, and swung. My wood collided against his with a crack. He kept his footing, but I shuffled back two steps. He raised his weapon and hacked at me from right to left over and over. I blocked each blow, backpedaling even further, unable to get myself out of his barrage. He was strong, and I was quickly losing any chance of gaining the upper hand.

"You are weak," he growled, stepping back and tossing his weapon from one hand to the other. "A daughter of Strong Haven should never be so."

He was toying with me.

Strong Haven was the Faevenly province my

mother was from, but my father was a human and was born and raised in Austin, Texas. I had a huge family here, while I had none in Faevenly. I didn't think anyone over there remembered me.

"I may be a daughter of Strong Haven, but I am also a daughter of the Avilas from Texas."

The fae stepped closer, his stick ready for another onslaught. "Humans are lesser beings. It would do you well to not forget the power of the fae bloodline running through your veins."

Grabbing the first thing I saw to my left, I chucked a picture frame at him. The shiny wood with a gold leaf pattern soared through the air on a path straight for his face. The fae snatched it from its course with ease and set it down on the entry table.

"Tsk, tsk, tsk," he taunted, then pointed his stick at me. "Use your weapon, girl."

"Fine," I muttered, advancing quickly with a jab.

He swung back. I used my short height to my advantage and ducked with ease, narrowly missing his swipe by a hair. Quickly catching my balance, I spun around to ram him in the gut, but he easily maneuvered out of the way.

His lip curled. "Fae are ruthless, vengeful, and manipulative. We cannot lie, but we do not need to because we are cunning and devious. We are immortal, but not impervious to being killed. We are incredibly strong, but fall down to iron."

"A lesson?" I kept my stick pointed at him and backtracked toward the stairs. If I could get to higher ground, I could best him. I just needed to keep him talking. "You are attacking me, and you want to give me a lesson?"

He furrowed his brow in anger. "You obviously have a lot to learn," he hissed.

My heel met the first step of the stairs, but a basket blocked my way. Served me right for not putting my stuff away when Mom asked. I had to redirect my path, and quickly. My attacker looked ready to pounce.

He sneered. "If you give a fae your name, you give away your power. If a fae causes you to not know your name, you lose all sense of yourself. If a fae's name is hidden and you know what it is, you can use it against the fae."

He swung at my legs and I jumped, but not high enough. I toppled over in a heap, narrowly missing the wood entryway table. And then I glanced at my nails. I had just gotten a manicure two days earlier, and two of my nails were chipped.

"Great," I muttered, lowering my weapon. "You made me ruin my nails." He paused for a second. Before he could attack again, I blurted, "I give, Uncle Leto. You win."

He raised his brow, then lowered his weapon and placed it back where it belonged. "So soon? We did not even make it out of this room. You used to give me a real challenge."

I held out my hand, waving for him to help me up, and he pulled me to my feet with ease. "I haven't seen you in a while, so I'm rusty."

"Rusty indeed," he chuckled.

I leaned my stick against the wall. "Where've you been anyway? You haven't been by in a long time. And why all the fae lessons?"

When I was little, we crossed over to Faevenly all the time, using the shimmery portal my mom and dad had. Eventually, we stopped going because stuff kept us away—school, sports, my parents' bakery that now had three locations across Austin. As much as I loved visiting Uncle Leto and Aunt Pen, our life was earth-bound, not fae bound.

Besides, Faevenly didn't need us.

"I apologize for my lengthy absence, young princess. Faevenly has kept me and Aunt Pen quite busy. As for the lesson," he paused, "I wanted to make sure you had not forgotten who you are."

A twinge of guilt struck me, because he was right. I had forgotten one or two of those points, but I didn't want to admit it. "Of course I haven't forgotten, Uncle. How could I?"

Leto was tall and slender, over six feet with long, silver hair. I didn't really know his age because fae aged slowly, but he looked to be in his thirties or so. Though he was probably more like three or four hundred years old. My mom aged slowly too, but had started taking a serum when she crossed over to the human realm so she could match my dad's life span. They were both eighteen when they met. Now they were almost forty.

"Well, can I get a hug?" I asked, moving in for one

because we hugged in the Avila family. It was a whole thing.

"Always." He smiled.

He wrapped his arms around me and squeezed. He smelled like the fae realm—earthy, wild, and faintly sweet—a scent I'd almost forgotten but instantly recognized. Before we broke away, my phone beeped.

"Sorry, Uncle Leto. That's probably my cousin Aliana. I'm meeting her at the coffee shop to study for a big test." I drew back and peeked at my phone to check. "Yep, it's her."

He frowned. "The human realm keeps you busy doing useless things. I ought to know, I used to live here."

"Come on, now. My grades aren't useless. They're important for getting into college, and I really need to do well on this test."

He crossed his arms. "Say whatever you will, young princess, but I know better." He leaned forward. "Useless."

I laughed, then added, "Whatever you say, old wise one."

He kept a stoic stare on me before smiling. "Now, will you please contact your mother and father and tell them I am here for a visit? I require their presence posthaste."

"Posthaste?" I started texting my mom. "Is everything okay?"

He paused before saying, "All is as it should be."

As he has so aptly reminded me, fae could never

lie, but they were clever with their words. And there was something about his answer that told me he was hiding something.

"'All is as it should be' sounds like everything is messed up," I said. "Everything okay with you?"

He clasped his hands in front of his body and nodded. "I am well."

"Is it Aunt Pen? Everything okay with her?"

He nodded again. "She is well."

My phone beeped and I glanced at the text. Mom and Dad were headed over. Then I texted Aliana to tell her I'd be late. I wanted to spend time with my Uncle, at least until my parents arrived.

"Okay," I announced, slipping my phone in my jeans pocket. "Mom and Dad are on their way, and I texted my cousin that I'd be late. So I'm all yours for a little while. How about we catch up over some tea?"

He smiled. "Tea with my favorite young princess sounds wonderful."

He followed me into the kitchen and took a seat at the table. I started filling the teapot with water. "So, Uncle Leto, how long has it been?" My mind shuffled through the years in my head. "Two or three—"

"Four years," he said.

"Four? Really?" I set the pot on the burner of our gas stove and turned the knob. The flame ignited with a small spark. "No way."

He crossed one leg over the other and sat back in his chair. "The last time I was here, you were nearly in your first year of high school and had discovered the fencing team. Your mother and I practiced with you under a warm sun, then enjoyed a family meal your father and Aunt Pen made."

The events of that day sprang to my mind. Uncle Leto, Mom, and I spent hours outside practicing with my new fencing swords and gear while Dad showed Aunt Pen the ins and outs of barbecue. Even though I was a highly skilled sword and dagger fighter after all my lessons with Mom, I still practiced like a fiend because the fencing equipment was so different from the real thing.

"All that fencing gear was so clunky, but I caught on pretty quick." I opened the cupboard and brought out several tea bags, remembering how proud I was that afternoon, and how much fun we all had. I placed the bags on a tray along with two floral-patterned cups and saucers.

"A natural," he said. "You have your fae bloodline to thank for that."

"Yeah, that was a great time." I poured the hot water into the cups, then sat across from him. We started dunking our bags and I found myself marveling at the gracefulness of his long hands. They reminded me of my mother's.

"Are you still fencing?" he asked. Or have you taken up softball? You had quite the swing with that stick."

I sat up straighter, proud of the way I had whacked at him. "I did, didn't I?"

He nodded. "You did indeed."

"Well, as great as I am with my swing, I'm all in

with fencing. I'm the team captain now. I'm hoping to get signed by a college, too. I should know something in the next few months."

"That is lovely, young princess." He took a sip of tea, his mind suddenly looking far away.

I was about to probe him about Faevenly when the back door opened. Mom wore a happy yet worried expression as she took quick steps to the kitchen table. Dad just looked worried.

They were dressed in jeans and white T-shirts with the bakery logo on the front pocket—Wonder Waffles and More. Even though they had three stores and didn't need to work anymore, they did anyway—at the flagship location—because they loved it.

"Oh, Traeliorn," Mom said. "It is so wonderful to see you." Uncle Leto's full name was Traeliorn Letormis, but Dad and I called him Leto for short.

"Celyse." He stood with a smile and the two hugged.

When they separated, Dad went in for a hug too, clapping the tall fae on the back. "Good to see you, Leto." He looked about. "No Pen?"

"No, no Pen," he said. "This is not a social visit."

Mom furrowed her brow slightly, then glanced from Uncle Leto to Dad. "I see."

"Gabriela." Dad cleared his throat. "Will you give us some privacy?"

"Oh," I muttered, surprised at the request because Mom and Dad shared everything with me. At least, I thought they did. "Um, sure."

My phone beeped again. It was Aliana, asking where I was. I texted her I'd be on my way, then said a round of goodbyes.

As I stepped outside, that same sense of dread I had felt earlier crept up my spine. Whatever Uncle Leto was telling my parents had to be bad. There was no other explanation for the unease coursing through my veins.

The feeling didn't fade as I walked to my car. It stayed there, low and constant, like a warning humming beneath my skin.

I paused with my hand on the door handle and glanced back at the house. Everything looked the same —the porch light glowing, the curtains drawn, shadows settling in like they always did.

But something felt... off. Like I had already missed something important. Like whatever was coming had already started.

The dark, cold coffee shop oozed with the aroma of freshly ground coffee and buzzed with jazz and chatter. Yet my unease from earlier stuck to me like glue. If anything, it had settled deeper, like something waiting. Glancing around for Aliana, I spotted her at our usual booth in the back. Her petite hand waved me over.

"You made it," she said with a smile, pushing her thick black-framed glasses up the bridge of her nose.

She had skin a few shades lighter than mine, earning her the nickname of *guera* when we were growing up. She kept her curly hair short and wore one side tucked behind her ear and the other side loose. We did everything together and had been in the same class since kindergarten. Back then, she was a savior of sorts. All the kids made fun of me because I had long dark hair full of white streaks, and because my *abuela*, my dad's mom, was a *curandera*. They called me *bruja* and used to make the sign of the cross whenever I walked by.

Eventually, the voices of my bullies dimmed until finally, when I entered high school, they vanished altogether because that's when I morphed into someone new.

With my burgeoning fencing skills, my heavy black eyeliner, and a thick "I don't care" attitude, not to mention the curves that had erupted at my hips and my chest, I started getting a different kind of attention. Girls wanted to hang out with me and guys wanted to date me. Even so, I mostly kept to myself. If I wasn't with Aliana, I was alone. I preferred it that way. Control was easier when I kept my distance.

"Yeah, sorry." I slipped into the small booth and set my stuff on the table. "My Uncle Leto paid us a surprise visit, and we were catching up."

"Your uncle with the long white hair?" She leaned in and whispered. "From the fae realm?"

When an evil fae witch destroyed my *abuela's* house, everything unraveled at once—or so I'd been told. In the chaos, my dad and his best friend, my Uncle Manny, vanished into Faevenly. After that, the family did what they could to hold it together while they searched for them. It was my dad's senior year of high school. They were my age. The thought left a chill in my chest. Everyone in the family knew about my mom. And somehow, they managed to keep the truth hidden.

"Yes," I whispered. "Him."

Her big eyes grew bigger. "You haven't mentioned your mom's family in forever. Is everything okay?"

I blew out a breath and rubbed the back of my

neck. "I don't know. I've got this weird vibe I can't figure out." And I didn't like not understanding it.

"Uh-oh." She swallowed. "A vibe like your dad gets?"

I shrugged. "Maybe. I dunno. It's hard to explain."

"Try," she prodded, eager to hear more. "I need details, *prima*."

Aliana was a total nerd and always had her nose buried in books about dragons and elves. She loved anything and everything having to do with fantasy and the paranormal, which for me was real life. She always wanted to know more about my mom and dad.

I thought for a moment about what to say to her, because I hardly understood it myself. "Most of the time when I have a bad feeling, there's an explanation. Like a creepy dead person trying to get my attention. Or a car crash I had just barely missed." I rubbed my head, trying to decipher this unique vibe. "But the feeling I'm having now is different. It started before I went inside my house and discovered Uncle Leto, and it hasn't really left me yet. It's in the background of my mind." Like it was trying to get my attention.

She tilted her head. "So, the bad vibe is... your uncle?"

"No, not him. But I think it's whatever news he has for my parents." I scooted closer to her and said in the lowest of voices, "I'm pretty sure something is up in Faevenly."

Her lips made the shape of an O. She held them like that before saying, "That's, like, bad, isn't it?"

"Hey, Aliana. Hey, Gabriela."

We jumped, and Aliana let out a squeak. It was Carlos standing at our table and looking down on us. He was tall and skinny with a wild 'fro, and we'd known him forever.

"Carlos!" She swatted his arm. "You can't sneak up on people like that!"

"Sneaking? Who's sneaking? I just came over here to say hi." He scooted in next to Aliana, then leaned over like we had been doing. "So, what are we talking about?" he asked in a whisper.

I put my hand on his forehead and gave him a playful push. "Nothing that concerns you."

"Hey," he retorted. "No need to get physical." He scooted closer to Aliana, turning his attention to her. "Your cousin is so rude."

"I'm only rude when people bother me," I said with a laugh. "And also, when I need coffee. Y'all want anything?"

"No, thanks," Aliana said.

"I'm good," Carlos added.

With my wallet in hand, I scooted out of the booth as a sharp tingle struck the back of my neck. I placed my hand on the table and steadied myself.

"Gabriela?" Aliana touched my wrist. "You all right?"

Resisting the urge to rub my neck, I gave myself a few seconds, then patted her hand. "Yep, I'm fine. Nothing coffee can't fix."

Find the source.

Turning away from them, I scanned the coffee shop looking for a spirit or other sign of trouble, when a guy with long dark hair in a thick braid and dressed in jeans and a black hoodie caught my eye.

He was sitting at a table in the corner of the coffee shop by the door. With his body angled away from me, I couldn't see his face. But something about him held my attention. Not curiosity—something sharper.

I left Aliana and Carlos and wove my way around the tables, heading for the counter while keeping my eye on the guy. His long legs were stretched out and crossed at the ankles. He sipped his coffee slowly, his movements slow and precise. I wondered who he was and what he was up to, especially since he didn't have a book or laptop with him.

The line at the counter wasn't long, only three people deep, and I took my place. I shuffled from side to side, trying not to be too obvious about watching the guy. Was he simply hanging out by himself and enjoying a cup of coffee? I mean, who does that?

There was something off about him. Not just that he was alone—but the way he sat, too still, like he was waiting for something.

A chill slipped down my spine. For a second, I had the strange feeling he knew I was watching him. Then he stood. He pushed his chair in, slipped his hands in his jean pockets, and left.

My stare trailed his movement through the glass, watching as he walked down the sidewalk and disappeared from view. The feeling didn't fade with him.

"Hello?" the barista said loudly, snapping her gum. "Do you want to order something?"

"Sorry," I said hastily, scooting up to the counter. "I'll take an iced vanilla latte with oat milk."

"Your name?"

"Gabriela."

She scribbled on a piece of paper, then handed me my receipt. I mumbled a thanks and stood to the side. When I got my drink, I went back over to Aliana. She was sitting alone, and I saw that Carlos had gone back to where his friends were.

"Hey," I said, slowly lowering myself to the seat. "Did you happen to see that guy by the door with jeans and a hoodie and long hair braided hair?"

She sat up and eyed the front of the coffee shop. "I don't see anyone."

"He's gone now," I said. "I was just wondering if you saw him."

"Was he hot?" she asked.

I laughed. "I don't know. I couldn't see his face. But maybe?"

Pushing my worries away, and with the tingling at the back of my neck almost gone, Aliana and I got busy studying. Over the next two hours, I labored over calculus. When I finished my last problem, I thought Uncle Leto was right. Math and tests and maybe even school were completely useless.

When I got home, I tossed my stuff by the front door and found Mom and Dad in the living room. Dad sat on the couch and Mom sat facing him, their bodies angled and their knees touching. I don't think my parents were ever together without touching.

"Hey, *mija*," Dad said when I entered the room. "How'd it go with studying?"

"It was fine." I flopped down on the blue plush chair in the corner. "Uncle Leto said school is useless, and he might be right." I glanced about. "Where is he, anyway?"

Mom shifted away from Dad. "He has gone back to Faevenly."

My back straightened. "So soon?"

Mom and Dad exchanged a look. The kind that said they had something bad to tell me. My stomach turned. The vibe I'd been feeling hadn't completely gone away.

"What is it?" I asked in a low voice. "It's something bad, isn't it? I've been tingling for hours."

"You have?" Mom asked, her hand lightly touching Dad's knee in that worried way.

"Yeah, I felt it when I got home from school, and then again at the coffee shop. Even a little bit now."

A serious expression covered Dad's stubbled face. "Did you notice anything out of the ordinary today? See any spirits?"

My mind flashed to the guy in the hoodie. I thought of mentioning him, but quickly decided against it. It was nothing. Besides, seeing a guy in a hoodie at a coffee shop was an everyday occurrence.

"No spirits, and nothing out of the ordinary," I said. "Why?"

A stretch of silence filled the room before Mom explained. "Uncle Leto brought news of unrest in Faevenly. He has asked your father and me to attend an upcoming meeting of the Council of Six. He thinks our presence will help calm things."

I blinked. "Unrest?" The word settled wrong in my chest, like it meant more than they were saying. "What kind of unrest?"

"Power struggles amongst the provinces," Mom answered.

"Wait, what?"

My brain quickly recalled the politics of Faevenly. Forever ago, like centuries, it was divided into seasonal courts, but then the Strong family, my mom's family, claimed ultimate rule and renamed the seasonal courts into provinces—Strong Haven and a few others I couldn't remember. Though I did remember my mom telling me about an area with rocks and caverns called the Sublands.

I scooted up to the edge of my seat. "I know I need to brush up on my fae history, but wasn't a power struggle the reason why you left Faevenly with Dad all those years ago? A struggle that caused a lot of deaths?"

Mom shifted closer to Dad. "There was and there were, but this is nothing like that."

"It's only a meeting," Dad tacked on. "We'll be gone for a week. Possibly less."

It was clear they were going no matter what I said, and I couldn't blame them. Faevenly was Mom's home.

She was still a princess and a daughter of Strong Haven, even if she didn't live there anymore.

"Fine. I'm coming with y'all."

"No, ma'am," Dad said sharply, his tone cutting me off like a slap in the face. "You are staying here and going to school, and that's final."

"But Dad, I haven't been to Faevenly in a long time. If y'all have to go, then this will be a perfect time for me to reconnect. I'm a daughter of Strong Haven, after all, and I should—"

"No!" Dad said again. He eased back and rubbed his forehead, calming himself. "Please, *mija*. It has to be this way."

With a sinking feeling in my gut, I waited a few seconds before I asked, "When are y'all going?"

"Tomorrow," Mom answered. "In the morning."

"Tomorrow?" I repeated. It was all so sudden.

"Yes," Mom said. "We will be back before you know it."

I cleared my suddenly dry throat. "Will y'all be in any danger? Should I be worried?"

"No danger, and no worry," Dad answered, but a slight quiver of Mom's lip told me otherwise. What were they not telling me?

"So what's the plan?" I asked.

"*Abuela* Alicia is coming over in the morning," Dad explained. "She'll be staying here with you until we get back. Uncle Manny will be minding the bakeries. He'll be looking in on you too."

Since I wasn't going to get any info from Mom or

Dad, or change their minds, I decided to accept what was happening and retreat to my room. "If that's settled, then I guess I'll see y'all in the morning."

Dad glanced at Mom before saying, "Yes, it's settled."

Leaving them, I scooped up my things, got a glass of water, then went upstairs for a long hot shower and went to bed earlier than usual. Snuggled under my soft white comforter, I turned to my side and gazed out my window. The light from the full moon outside cast a soft glow around the edges of my window blinds. I let out a long breath, then rubbed the back of my neck, telling myself over and over not to worry.

Mom was born and raised in Faevenly. Uncle Leto, Aunt Pen, Maid Gidna, and the Strong Haven healer, Lady Sonia, were there. Not to mention a full regiment of Strong Haven guards. The realm was beautiful and peaceful, and everything was going to be fine.

So why did it feel like I was lying to myself?

CHAPTER 3

My eyes were sealed shut when my alarm started playing at seven in the morning. The feeling from yesterday lingered, faint but impossible to ignore. With a lunge, I grabbed my phone from my nightstand and slammed my fingers down, hoping one of them hit the snooze button. When the music finally silenced, I rolled over and burrowed under my covers. I needed five more minutes.

"Gabriela?" Mom's voice carried into my room, drifting over me like a soothing whisper. "Your father and I are leaving."

Her words floated around my head before finally sinking in. "You are?" I mumbled, peeling my eyes open. I knew they were leaving today, but didn't think it'd be this early. "Right now?"

"Yes, right now," she said.

Peering up at them, I saw that Mom wore a long flowy green dress that matched her green eyes. Dad stood behind her and wore dark pants with a long-sleeved white button-down shirt. A fresh shave revealed a smooth and chiseled face.

"Wow, y'all look nice," I mumbled.

"Thank you, my love," Mom said. She leaned over and kissed my forehead. "We will see you when we get back, okay?"

"Yeah, okay."

Dad squeezed my foot. "*Abuela* Alicia is excited to be here. She's downstairs making *migas*."

My stomach growled. "She is?" I loved *Abuela* Alicia's food, and hadn't had her *migas* in a long time.

"Yes." He smiled. "She is."

Suddenly, them leaving and *Abuela* staying didn't sound so bad. "Well, don't hurry back, then."

Dad chuckled. "Hey, now." Then he leaned over and kissed my forehead like mom had.

When they left my room, I snuggled back into my pillow, listening to their footsteps against the wood floor as they walked down the hall and then down the stairs. Their voices, mixed with *Abuela*'s, drifted through the house. A few minutes later, the back door opened, then closed.

I dragged myself out of bed, went to my window, and lifted the slats of my blinds. I watched them walk into the wooded area behind our house until they slipped out of view between the trees. Something about them leaving so early didn't sit right.

Out in the trees is where Mom would open her shimmery portal to Faevenly, a round glowing orb she kept hidden. When I was little, I used to ask her all the time where she kept it, but she never told me. Which made sense. Back then I probably would've found it and used it and gotten into a whole lot of trouble.

It is in a safe place, my love. And if you ever need it, you will find it.

The years had made me forget about the shimmer. But now, I wondered where Mom and Dad had stored it. I yawned as I imagined where they possibly kept such a thing when my alarm sounded again. The tune pulled me away from my thoughts and prodded me into action. I needed to get ready for school.

Sliding my feet into my fluffy black slippers, I glanced at my reflection in the mirror. Dark, puffy circles encased my eyes, and my long hair twisted in frizzy knots.

"Great," I muttered. "I look the way I feel."

"Gabriela!" *Abuela* called out. "Breakfast will be ready soon!"

I opened my door and leaned out. "Be down in thirty minutes!"

I hurried to the bathroom and started getting ready as fast as I could. I yanked my brush through my hair, lined my eyes with dark eyeliner, swept some brown eyeshadow on my eyelids, and dabbed my cheeks with highlighter. Back in my room, I slipped on my dark jeans and a green shirt, finishing my look with my gold hoop earrings. With the delicious aroma of *migas* beckoning me, I grabbed my backpack and keys and trotted downstairs.

"*Mira mi hermosa Gabriela,*" *Abuela* said with a big smile. "So beautiful."

"Good morning, *Abuela.*"

She was short and thin with long silver hair kept in

a low ponytail. Deep lines accentuated her eyes and lips, and the aroma of herbs and spice from the cuttings she used in her oils and salves hung around her like her own personal brand of earthy perfume.

She was a famous *curandera*, or healer, and people came to see her from all over for life advice and remedies. She also helped people communicate with spirits to say goodbye or ask questions. But the coolest stuff she did was help solve mysteries and crimes. Once, she helped the FBI locate a kidnapped boy. She became an instant celebrity but hated the attention. It died down after a while, though every now and again the FBI would reach out to her for help.

"*En español, por favor,*" she demanded with a look.

My Spanish was awful, so she always made me use it with her. Which I actually appreciated. I was half Hispanic and didn't speak Spanish nearly as well as I should have.

"*Buenos días, Abuela,*" I said, appeasing her.

With a satisfied smile, she started asking me about school and friends and fencing. I muddled through my responses in Spanish while I dug into my *migas,* both savoring and rushing through each bite of fluffy egg and crunch of corn tortilla. I was running late.

When I finished, I set my dish in the sink and hugged her. "*Gracias, Abuela.* But I gotta *vamos.*"

She corrected my Spanish while shooing me out the door with a dishrag. Scuttling away from her, I hopped in the car and took off. If I didn't hurry, I'd have to park in the school's back lot. Nobody wanted to park there because that meant getting stuck behind the buses at the end of the day. And sure enough, that's where I ended up.

"Great," I muttered, taking the last spot. I was way later than I thought. I didn't even see anyone else parking.

I hopped out of my car, backpack in tow, when a tingle slammed me against my car. I stayed there, stunned, fear flooding every inch of me because a bad vibe had never done that before. And then another force slammed into me from behind. But this one was made of flesh and bone. A pair of strong hands wrestled my backpack off of me, but before the thief could get away, I spun around and grabbed the straps, yanking him to a halt.

My eyes widened when he turned around. He wasn't just a regular thief. He was a fae. Pointy ears protruded through his long black hair, and deadly dark eyes bored into me.

"Foolish daughter of Strong Haven," he hissed through elongated teeth.

My blood ran cold as I gasped. *A fae vampire*?

Every defensive move I knew vanished as pure, utter fear gripped me like a vise. *Move,* I told myself. *Do something.* But I couldn't. I could barely think. Mom and Dad had never mentioned a fae creature like him before. What else had they not mentioned?

I dropped my strap. "You're a f-f-fae v-v-vampire."

A whoosh sounded as an arrow flew by my face. It lodged through the fae's head, entering above his eyebrow and sticking out the back of his skull. His face went slack as he released my backpack, then slowly toppled onto me. I stumbled, my voice mixed between a grunt and a scream as I tried to push him off of me but couldn't. He was too heavy.

Another figure swooped in. Fast. Precise. Controlled. I braced for a blow when I recognized the guy from the coffee shop, or at least I thought it was him. He had the same physique and long dark ponytail. He grabbed my attacker by the shoulders, pulled him off of me, and dropped him to the ground. Like he'd done it a hundred times before.

I grasped the collar of my shirt and bunched it up in my hand, my breathing quick and shallow as I stared at the fae vampire on the floor. Panic flooded me, my mind racing in a million different directions. This was connected to my parents and Faevenly. It had to be. And it was no coincidence that the guy from the coffee shop was here.

He placed his hand on my shoulders. I tore my gaze away from the body on the asphalt and looked up at him. He had long black hair that hung loose at his shoulders, porcelain-smooth ivory skin, and sparkling blue eyes. The tips of his ears were barely noticeable, but he was a fae, all right. And he was beautiful.

He didn't look shaken, not even a little. "Are you hurt?" His voice was calm and smooth.

I did a quick mental assessment of my body and didn't detect any physical injuries. "No," I muttered. "I-I-I'm not."

He looked down at the dead fae, then back up at me. Like death didn't faze him, like he was used to it. "Go straight home, right now. I will handle this."

The late bell blared through the parking lot, jarring me to my senses. A dead fae vampire lay at my feet, and a fae who'd obviously been following me had killed him.

"You were at the coffee shop," I muttered.

"I was. My name is Leaf, and I am here to help you." He leaned down so his face was even with mine. "Lord Letormis asked me to watch over you while your mother and father went to Faevenly."

I blinked. "My Uncle Leto?"

"Yes. Now please, you need to leave so I can handle this before someone sees what has happened."

"Handle what?" I shot back, my voice sharper than I expected.

"Something you don't need to see," he said evenly.

Glancing around, I saw a couple of stragglers dashing to the back entrance of the school. It was only a matter of time before someone came by and noticed us.

Leaf picked up my backpack and handed it to me. I took it with caution, still unsure of who he was, but convinced he was right. I needed to get out of there.

"Okay," I swallowed. I took a step toward my car but then stopped. "What are you going to do with...?" I gestured lamely to the body on the ground. And suddenly it was starting to sink in that there was a *body* on the ground next to me.

"I will dispose of the creature and then I will come to your house." He placed his hand under my chin, bringing my attention back to those eyes. Once he apparently saw what he needed, his hand trailed from my chin to my elbow as he ushered me to my car door, his touch gentle yet firm. "Now please, you must go."

With a nod, I reached for the handle, but my hands were shaking so violently I couldn't get a grip. He reached in smoothly. "Here, let me."

I dropped my hand, and he opened the door. I lowered myself into the car and he closed the door behind me. I cranked the ignition, my body trembling all over, and slowly pulled out of my spot. My stomach twisted so tight I could heave.

"Just breathe," I told myself. "Breathe, breathe, breathe." This wasn't over. It couldn't be.

I wove my way out of the lot and drove on autopilot to my house. I didn't live too far away, but in my state of mind it took forever for me to get there. Finally, I reached my house. I hadn't been parked for more than a second when *Abuela* ran out of the house and straight for me. I quickly got out of the car and she threw her surprisingly strong, petite arms around me.

"*¡Mija!*" she exclaimed before jabbering in Spanish so fast and with such strong emotion I couldn't catch most of what she was saying. But I was able to decipher that she had felt something was wrong and was worried when I didn't answer my phone.

"I'm okay," I choked out.

She pulled back and cupped my face with her warm, wrinkly hands. "*Dígame.* What happened, *mija*?"

My hands wouldn't steady. "A fae attacked me in the school parking lot. Another fae showed up and"—I paused while the scene flashed in my mind—"killed him. He told me to come home right away and said he'd meet me here after he got rid of the body. He said Uncle Leto sent him to watch over me while Mom and Dad went to Faevenly."

Abuela's eyes went from wide to furrowed and back to wide. She clasped me in another tight hug and held me for a long while. "Come," she said, rubbing my back. "Let us get inside."

We went inside and straight to the kitchen. *Abuela* filled the tea kettle and placed it on the stove. She rummaged through her bags, brought out a clear jar filled with small packets of her homegrown herbs, and set it on the counter next to two empty teacups.

"We will call your Uncle Manny while the water boils," she said with a reassuring nod.

"Okay," I muttered, wiping my face with a tissue, feeling completely dazed.

She took her phone and held it up to her ear. "*Manny, necesito que vengas a la casa de Julio. Rápidamente.*"

I heard the muffle of Uncle Manny's voice but couldn't make out what he was saying. A few seconds later, *Abuela* said goodbye and set the phone down.

"What did he say?" I asked.

"He said he is coming, *mija*."

The teapot whistled, prompting her to remove the kettle and fill the cups with steaming water. She unscrewed her jar and a symphony of scents—peppermint and lavender and other spices—filled the air. She took out two small herbal packets and dropped them into the hot water, then handed me the cup.

"Sip, *mija*," she encouraged. "It will help your nerves."

I brought the cup up to my nose and inhaled, breathing in the soothing aroma. I sipped the warm liquid and it slid down my throat with ease, instantly calming me. My shoulders relaxed and my stomach muscles loosened.

I had gone through this same tea drinking process with Uncle Leto just the day before. Now, my life was spinning out of control in a way I had never imagined. I'd seen a lot of spirits, bloodied and wounded, but nothing compared to seeing someone's life taken right before my eyes. Least of all a fae vampire. I never wanted to see something like that again. But what did it all mean? Why would anyone attack me?

Somehow, I knew it hadn't been random. This wasn't over. Whatever had come for me... it would come again.

She scooted in and started speaking in Spanish. But my rattled brain couldn't make out her words. "I'm sorry, but I can't translate right now."

"I was telling you to be calm and to work on your breathing. I can see you are holding your air."

"Oh," I said, not realizing I'd been holding my breath. "You're right."

Before I could exhale, the doorbell rang and I jumped in my seat. It was either Uncle Manny, the fae guy named Leaf, or the cops.

"Should I hide?" I whispered.

"No, of course not. You have done nothing wrong." She patted my hand. "You stay here and I'll answer the door."

Her small bare feet padded against the wood floor as she went to the door. Even though she told me not to hide, I tiptoed out of sight anyway. Just in case.

"I got here as soon as I could. Where is she?"

I blew out a sigh of relief hearing Uncle Manny's hurried voice. "I'm in the kitchen!" I called out.

Uncle Manny dashed in with *Abuela* on his heels. He was skinny and short with thick wavy dark hair, dark skin, and a goatee. He wasn't my uncle by blood, but may as well have been. He and my dad grew up together and were best friends, and I knew he'd do anything for me. He was also my *padrino*.

"Gabriela, are you okay?" He cupped my cheeks and studied my face, as if searching for an injury. "Are you hurt?"

I shook my head. "I'm fine. Nothing happened to me."

"Nothing nothing... or witchy nothing?"

Uncle Manny always called the family Avila talents "witchy." And they were. But in this case, other than getting a huge tingle right beforehand, I hadn't done anything. The fae had.

"Well," I said. "Not witchy, but fae-y."

He dropped his hands and looked from me to *Abuela*, a hint of fear flashing across his face. "The fae? What do you mean?"

"A fae guy knocked into me in the school parking lot and grabbed my backpack, and another fae guy shot him with an arrow in the head."

Uncle Manny sucked in a sharp breath. "Shot him? As in, dead?"

"Yes, dead," I answered.

"Dead dead?" he asked again.

I nodded.

He pinched the bridge of his nose and said, "This fae guy that came to your aid... did he tell you his name?"

"Yes, he said his name is Leaf and that Uncle Leto sent him to watch over me while Mom and Dad went to Faevenly."

"Leaf?" Uncle Manny's voice raised an octave. He quickly controlled himself and cleared his throat. "Leaf with long dark hair and blue eyes?"

"Yes," I swallowed, unsure how to take his reaction. "That's him. Why? Is something wrong with him? Do I need to be worried? He said he'd be coming here after he got rid of the dead fae guy."

Abuela set a cup of tea in front of Uncle Manny. He pushed it away and thrummed his fingers on the table.

"If Leto sent him, then no, there is nothing to worry about."

"Then what?" I asked. "You're kinda freaking me out right now, Uncle Manny."

"I want to know too," *Abuela* added. "Especially if this person is coming here."

Pain flashed in Uncle Manny's eyes, and it took him a few long seconds to figure out what to say. "Back when your father and I went through... everything we went through in Faevenly... Leaf was with us. He fought alongside us, but at times he was... complicated."

"Complicated?" I pressed. "Complicated how?"

The doorbell rang again, cutting our conversation short, and I was pretty sure it was Leaf. Uncle Manny ran his fingers through his thick hair and said in a quiet voice, "Listen, Gabriela, it doesn't matter. What your mom and dad and I went through back in Faevenly was a long time ago. The only thing that's important right now is your Uncle Leto sent Leaf to help. So if Leto can trust him, we can too."

I had no idea what to think about that, but I needed some sort of reassurance. "But he's a good guy, right?"

"Yes, he's a good guy."

I trusted Uncle Manny just like I trusted Uncle Leto. But in that moment, a sliver of doubt about Leaf worked its way into me. Even if he had saved my life, something was off about Leaf.

I would have bet my Avila witchyness on it.

CHAPTER 4

buela tossed her dishrag over her shoulder. "I agree with Manny. We trust Leto and his judgment. We have no other choice right now. So are we going to open the door for Leaf? Or are we going to leave him out there?"

She was right. We were stuck with having to trust Leaf because there was no real alternative. Especially since he had saved me from that fae vampire. Which reminded me, I hadn't mentioned that part to *Abuela* or Uncle Manny. I'd have to do that later. There was no time now.

We made our way to the door and Uncle Manny opened it with a grin. "Leaf!" he said in a friendly tone. "Come on in! It's great to see you!"

Um, really?

Uncle Manny was awkward and never knew how to act in delicate situations, so he overcompensated with friendliness. The kind of friendliness that was weird and cringey.

Leaf nodded with an air of formality. "Hello, Manny."

"Wow, you look fantastic, dude. But you know"—

he gave Leaf a wink and a nudge on the arm—"that is the fae way. Us humans get wrinkles and stuff."

I glanced at *Abuela*. She rolled her eyes at Uncle Manny, then stepped forward to take charge. "Leaf, I am Julio's mother, Alicia. Thank you so much for taking care of my granddaughter today at the school parking lot."

Leaf bowed his head. "It is very nice to make your acquaintance, Alicia. As for helping Lady Gabriela, I am honored."

"Please, come in," she beckoned.

"Yeah, where are my manners? Please come in, Leaf," Uncle Manny added with a laugh.

Keeping his hands clasped behind his back, Leaf took two steps in. His long and smooth jet-black hair flowed with each movement. He had abandoned his dark jeans and black hoodie and wore more fae-like attire—dark brown pants with a thick black belt and a long-sleeved dark green shirt. A bow and a quiver filled with arrows was strapped to his back, along with a fighting stick. He wore a holster at his hip with a long black onyx dagger. Full-blooded fae couldn't wield iron. Since I was only part fae, iron didn't bother me.

Leaf brought his attention to me, as if noticing me for the first time. "Lady Gabriela." His gaze lingered, sharp and unreadable, as if weighing something I couldn't see.

"What did you do with the body?" I blurted, my overwhelming need to know erasing my manners.

He raised a brow. His gaze flicked over me,

measured, before he finally said, "Your attacker was returned to Faevenly for proper handling."

Uncle Manny let out a sigh of relief. "Good. No body, no crime. Am I right?" He laughed again in that nervous way. "Thank you, Leaf."

"Of course," Leaf said.

With an awkward pause settling in, *Abuela* steered us out of the room with a wave. "Let's go to the kitchen. We have much to discuss."

Once in the kitchen, Leaf turned down the offer for tea. He also didn't want to sit. He stayed standing, feet wide, hands at his back, like a guard on duty. Uncle Manny paced around, clearly unsure if he should sit or stand. Finally, he leaned against the white quartz kitchen island.

"Leaf, we need answers," Manny said, taking on a serious tone. "First, Leto comes with a plea for Julio and Celyse to return to Faevenly for a special meeting. Then, without telling us, he leaves you here to watch over Gabriela. And this morning she gets attacked! What the hell is going on?"

"Uncle Leto should've prepared us," I added.

Abuela nodded her agreement, crossing her arms and studying Leaf with fierce intensity. She wanted answers too.

"I understand your concern. All of you," Leaf said, keeping his hands behind his back. "But Lord Letormis did not want to cause unnecessary alarm. I assure you he had the best intentions."

Uncle Manny glanced at me and *Abuela*, his eyes

telling us he believed Leaf. "I will never doubt Leto or his intentions. Not ever. We went through too much together for me to ever question him. But we need to know why Gabriela was attacked."

Leaf raised his chin in a defiant gesture. "I too will never doubt Lord Letormis. For the same reasons and more." He let his fiery stare stay with Uncle Manny a few seconds before toning it down.

Mom and Dad had told me the basics about what had happened to them so many years ago in Faevenly — Mom's family, the Strongs, were the rulers of Faevenly. She was bound to marry a fae but found a shimmery portal and met Dad. There were some betrayals, some fighting, some deaths, and then she left Faevenly and ended up staying in the human realm with Dad.

There were a lot more details Mom and Dad could have shared, but they never did. Now, I needed to know more. A lot more.

"Listen, I trust Uncle Leto too," I said. "But why would a fae come here and attack me?"

Leaf brought his stare to me, anger lacing his perfect features. "Princess Celyse abandoned her homestead for this lesser realm. Now, Strong Haven and all of Faevenly wavers."

"Hey, ease up there, Leaf," Uncle Manny said in a low, warning tone. "That's not at all a fair assessment, and you know that."

"I meant no disrespect," Leaf offered coolly. "My deepest apologies."

But I didn't think he was sorry at all.

Manny's phone beeped. He fumbled with it in his pocket, trying to silence it, but then it beeped three more times. "Sorry, everyone." He brought it out and read his texts with a frown, his fingers tapping as he replied to the message.

"Is everything okay? Do you need to go?" *Abuela* asked.

"I do, but in a minute. Let's finish here first." He rubbed his face, looking tired and old. Suddenly, I didn't really know Uncle Manny at all. What exactly did they all go through in Faevenly all those years ago? It had to have been way worse than any of them had let on.

"Leaf," he said. "Please explain what's going on in Faevenly and why Gabriela was attacked. We deserve the truth."

Leaf kept his formal stance with his chin slightly raised. "House Kane of High Meadow has been working against House Strong, gathering allies in an attempt to take the high court seat. They claim that without someone of Strong blood in the palace, the Strongs have no right to rule. They're challenging Lord Letormis's authority as ward of Strong Haven."

"That's great," Uncle Manny muttered. He started walking in circles. "Just great."

Someone wanting to take over the province was one thing, but crossing into the human realm and coming after me was another thing entirely. It didn't make sense.

"Okay, so there's a power struggle in Faevenly. I get that. But why would someone come over here and attack *me*? I'm no threat." With an apologetic look to *Abuela* and Uncle Manny, I added, "And I should probably mention that the fae who attacked me had pointy teeth, like a vampire."

Manny stopped in his tracks. He turned to face me, the blood draining from his face until he looked ashen. "Did you say vampire?"

His reaction chilled me through, and I found myself reaching out to hold *Abuela's* hand. "Yeah, he, uh, looked kinda like a vampire with long sharp teeth," I explained.

Abuela made the sign of the cross up and down her body and shoulder to shoulder. "*¿Es posible*, Manny? *Un fae vampiro*?"

Uncle Manny rubbed his face again. "Very possible. They're called soul vamps. But they don't suck blood; they suck souls, and the souls give them strength."

A shudder rocked my body. My parents had never mentioned a creature like that. "A soul vamp? That sounds terrifying."

"It is terrifying," Uncle Manny echoed. He turned his attention to Leaf. "But I thought there was only one, and he was slumbering in a dungeon until he died."

"There is one slumbering in a dungeon. But you made an incorrect assumption," Leaf replied. "They are rare, but Draven the witch is not the only one."

Manny continued pacing while I moved closer to

Abuela. The idea of a deadly soul vamp being locked away in a dungeon made me feel slightly better, but not by much, because a different one had attacked me.

"But why did one come here and try to hurt me?" I asked.

"You are a Strong," Leaf said in a somewhat biting tone, "a fact which you seem to have completely forgotten. If the Kanes cannot win the necessary votes at the Council of Six, then their next move will be to eliminate the name."

Eliminating the name meant killing me and my mom. My stomach churned as I tightened my grip around *Abuela's* hand.

Uncle Manny muttered under his breath, quickening his pacing around the kitchen. "If they're after Gabriela, then we need to get her out of here." He paused his step and flashed Leaf a worried expression. "Wait a minute, what about Celyse?"

"Lord Letormis does not believe it will come to that," he said.

"It already came to that because Gabriela was attacked!" Uncle Manny looked angrier than I had ever seen him. Gone was the overly jovial man who answered the door. "We're talking about the fae here."

Leaf remained steady and cool. "The soul vamp I killed today was not sent to take Lady Gabriela's life; if he was, she would be dead. Which means he was sent as a watcher only, most probably gathering information. As for Princess Celyse, she and Julio knew the risks when they left. But I assure you they will have a full guard detail with them at all times while in Faevenly."

"What about Gabriela?" he asked, coming to a stop in front of Leaf. "Is she safe?"

"*I* am here to assure her safety."

Manny's phone dinged again, and then once more. He yanked it from his pocket and read the message. "Dammit," he muttered. "I've got a conference out of town this weekend for the bakery and they're confirming. It's a huge deal for the company."

"Go on," *Abuela* said. "You are needed. We will be fine here with Leaf, and you can come back when you are finished."

Uncle Manny sighed, looking conflicted about what he should do, but then gave in to his responsibilities. "I'll go for the first day only. And I'll be back tomorrow night." He hugged me and *Abuela* at the same time. "And when I return, we can figure this all out. And please, Gabriela, do not leave this house. Okay?"

"Don't worry, I won't," I assured him. I had no intention of putting myself at risk. Not with creatures like soul vamps out there.

He nudged his chin in Leaf's direction. "Walk me to my car please?"

Leaf followed Manny out of the kitchen and to the front door. *Abuela* shooed me after them. "Go listen," she whispered.

She didn't have to tell me twice. When they were out of sight, I made my move, slowly creeping my way to the front door so they couldn't see me. Once they were outside, I scuttled forward and pressed my ear against the door.

"I don't know what the hell is going on, but nothing, and I mean nothing, better happen to Gabriela and *Abuela* Alicia while I'm gone. Got it?" Uncle Manny demanded.

"That is why I am here, Manny. I am charged with their safety in the human realm until Julio and Princess Celyse return. I am the strongest warrior in Faevenly. I will not fail."

Uncle Manny let out an exasperated huff. He said something else, but I couldn't make it out. I pressed my ear harder against the wood door, but only heard silence. And then the door swung open. I teetered forward and face planted into Leaf's chest. The hard body beneath his shirt jarred me with a smack, and the pleasing smell of spice and woods filled my nose. A flush spread across my cheeks, and I righted myself as quickly as I could.

His lips parted slightly and I thought I detected a small bob at his throat while he quickly pulled his gaze from my low cut shirt. "My apologies, Lady Gabriela."

I increased the distance between us. "Gabriela," I corrected. "I prefer you call me just Gabriela, please."

He stayed outside the threshold and nodded. "As you wish, Gabriela." He clasped his hands behind his back as if waiting for me to say or do something.

I stepped to the side. "You can come in."

He kept his place. "I was only coming to tell you

and your grandmother that I will be outside watching over the house."

He gave me a low nod, then turned and walked away. I tilted my head, staring as he strode out of view, unable to figure him out at all. On the one hand, he had protected me in the parking lot; on the other hand, he seemed almost angry about it.

Abuela came up beside me. "*¿A dónde va?*" She asked, looking around for him.

"*No sé,*" I muttered. "He said he would watch the house and then he walked away."

Abuela and I stood there for a while before we returned to the kitchen. She slid her dishrag from her shoulder and started frantically cleaning, which was what she did whenever she was stressed. I helped, picking up the cups and saucers and setting them in the sink. I was at risk, and so were my mom and dad. And a fae with an attitude was outside watching over us.

"I don't know what to think about him," I confessed to *Abuela*, turning on the hot water and sudsing the sponge.

"I know. *Yo también.* There are many emotions swirling inside of him," she said with a heavy sigh. "I cannot separate his thoughts."

I finished washing one of the cups and handed it to her. "You can sense what he is feeling and thinking?"

"Yes, but only in part," she said. "He's built walls within himself, and he doesn't even see them."

"What do we do?" I asked, turning to her, fresh

doubt about Leaf creeping in. "I feel like we should be doing something."

The lines on her face deepened and her shoulders looked tight. "We wait for your Uncle Manny to get back. Then we figure out our next move."

I nodded, but the unease inside me wouldn't settle. Waiting suddenly felt like the most dangerous thing we could do.

CHAPTER 5

After we cleaned the kitchen, I got my things and retreated upstairs to my room because there was nothing else I could do. Surrounded by my soft violet walls, I lowered myself onto the bed, my mind grappling with everything that had happened. It was still early morning, and yet it seemed like hours had passed. Aliana was probably wondering where I was. I fished my phone out of my bag. Sure enough, she'd been texting.

Aliana: Where are you?

Aliana: Hello?

Aliana: Worried. Text me asap

I gulped, feeling guilty about missing her messages. I texted back that I was home and okay. I didn't have to wait long for her to reply.

Aliana: Thank goodness. I was freaking out. Why are you home?

Me: Something came up

Aliana: Everything ok?

My attack in the parking lot flashed before my eyes and I thought of Leaf—mysterious, deadly, and complicated. Not to mention strikingly gorgeous. But mostly, he looked like he hated me. I wanted to tell her all about it, but knew it would be better to explain face to face. But if she came over, did that mean she'd be at risk? Maybe it was best if I didn't mention anything.

Me: Actually, I'm feeling sick

Aliana: Oh no! Sorry, *prima*!

Me: I'll be fine after I rest. Text me after school

Aliana: Ok

Putting my phone away, and with the stress of the morning exhausting me, I turned off my lights and closed my window blinds, then snuggled under my blanket to take a nap. Instead of finding slumber, my mind went back to the school parking lot, dissecting every second of what happened to me, when I realized something. The fae vampire that attacked me in the parking lot wasn't attacking *me*. He was after my backpack.

Flinging off my blanket, I got up, grabbed my backpack, and placed it on my bed. If he risked exposure to get it... it had to matter.

Unzipping it in a hurry, I inspected the contents—books, notebooks, my pencil bag, a calculator, and a tissue pouch. I shook out the contents to be sure I wasn't missing anything and found nothing out of the ordinary. Or I just didn't know what I was looking for.

With a swoop of my arm, I stuffed everything back in my bag, then tossed it onto the floor.

"What did he want?" I muttered to myself, sitting on my window seat.

My eyes drifted over my walls, roaming over the pictures of family and friends I had tacked to an over-sized cork board—my fencing teammates and me at a competition, the entire Avila family at Disney World, Aliana and me swimming in the lake.

A pathetic chuckle escaped my lips at the absurdity of thinking I could live a normal life. I was called a *bruja* when I was little because I was a *bruja*. I could see spirits and sense bad things like my dad and my *abuela*. Not to mention my mother wasn't even from this realm. Now, not only did fae soul vamps exist, but one had attacked me. There could be others who wanted me dead too, and it was all because my mom had left Faevenly.

There was no such thing as normal for me. There never had been. I'd just been pretending.

I opened my blinds. The silver-hued lake sparkled beneath the rays of the golden sun, and not a cloud could be seen in the bright blue sky. The day was perfect, while my life was anything but. I thought of Leaf keeping watch over me and *Abuela*. Where was he? Near the lake? Or maybe in the woods behind the house? I was sure he knew a lot more about what was going on in Faevenly than he had shared. And I was done waiting to find out.

I made my way downstairs and through the kitchen, where *Abuela* busily worked on her famous *caldo de res*. Cooking was another go-to activity for her when she was stressed. And I wasn't complaining. I loved her beef soup.

She glanced my way while cutting carrots. "Where are you going?"

Her tone suggested she wasn't going to approve of me going anywhere. Not that I blamed her. But I hoped she'd let me go outside. "Only to the patio so I can get some fresh air."

She held my gaze for a few long seconds. "Stay close to the house. *¿Entiendes?*"

"I will." Then I added, "*Prometo.*"

Being outside always made me feel better. The rustling of the trees filled me with immense peace. Sometimes I'd sit out back for hours listening to the sounds of nature. If I wasn't on the patio, I was on the dock, relaxing by the lake. But today, there was no calm for me. I cupped my hand over my eyes to shield the sunlight and scanned my tree-filled yard.

Leaf had to be around here somewhere.

"Leaf," I said, but not too loud for my *abuela* to hear. "Are you out here?" Fae could run fast and had excellent vision and sharp hearing. I was pretty sure he could hear me. "I want to talk to you."

He approached from the area by the lake, tall and beautiful, wearing an unreadable expression and striding with confidence. He stopped on the other side of the patio. "Gabriela, how may I be of service?"

I motioned to a pair of outdoor chairs. "Will you sit with me for a while?"

He hesitated a few seconds before saying, "Yes, I will sit with you."

We sat in silence, both of us staring off into the

distance. I started picking at my chipped nails while watching him from the corner of my eye. His posture was perfect, his back straight and his shoulders back. His features were chiseled, his lips full, and I didn't think I had ever seen such a flawless profile. But the most striking thing about him were his crystal-blue eyes and jet-black hair set against his porcelain skin.

"So, Leaf," I said, trying to figure out where I should start. "My Uncle Manny mentioned Draven the witch. Can you tell me about him?"

His jaw clenched and his hands tightened around his knees. "Draven is a powerful and devious soul vamp witch. He is responsible for much death and suffering in Faevenly."

"Oh," I swallowed. "Well, why is he like that?"

Leaf turned to face me with a fiery look in his eyes. "Draven is pure evil. He has always been so. He is power-hungry and devious and will do anything to exact revenge on those who have wronged him."

"Is that all?" I asked with a nervous laugh.

Leaf raised a brow and considered me with a hard look. "Are you jesting?"

"Oh, no," I explained quickly, realizing he wasn't getting the nuance of what I meant. "I mean, yeah, but no. It's my way of feeling not so terrified about something terrifying."

Leaf held my gaze in silence. He leaned closer to me. "You should not suppress your terror. It might keep you alive."

I hid a silent gulp, his warning scaring the hell out

of me, but his presence completely enrapturing me. He turned away from me and cast his gaze back on the woods.

"So, um, when you say exacting revenge, what do you mean exactly?"

He shook his head in exasperation. "Thundera-tion," he muttered under his breath. "You do not know anything, do you?" He rose to his feet, then hardened his gaze on mine. "You are caught up living a life of comfort and luxury, caring nothing about the havoc your family left in Faevenly. Your human side domi-nates everything about you, and you are useless."

My mouth fell open as I watched him walk away, my mind searching for some amazing comeback to throw at him but coming up empty. He was right. I had been so caught up in school, fencing, and friends that I never gave Faevenly a thought. I hadn't asked about Uncle Leto or Aunt Pen in years. Or Maid Gidna or Lady Sonia.

Guilt twisted deep inside my gut. Faevenly was where my mom was born and raised. It's where my mom and dad literally struggled against insurmount-able odds to be together. I should've taken more interest in what they had gone through. I should've asked more questions.

Leaf was right. I didn't know anything. I *was* totally and completely useless.

I pulled my legs up to my chest and wrapped my arms around my knees. When Mom and Dad returned,

I'd be ready to hear everything and ready to do whatever I could for Faevenly.

I just hoped it wouldn't be too late.

CHAPTER 6

I stayed outside while the day ticked by. The weather must've sensed my mood, because gray clouds slowly took over the blue sky. A chilly wind shook the trees, sending rustling leaves scattering down like a multicolored rainfall. Our small wind-chimes tinkled while our big ones gonged.

With a shiver settling into my bones, I retreated back inside and found myself enveloped by the savory smells of *caldo de res*. The hearty Mexican beef soup filled the kitchen with warmth, and my stomach growled in acknowledgment. I could practically taste the broth, chunks of meat, and all the savory vegetables.

Inside, with the promise of one of *Abuela's* delicious meals, everything felt infinitely better.

"Wow, that smells so good," I said, my mouth watering. "When will it be ready?"

Abuela smiled, stirring the large pot with her wooden spoon. "About thirty minutes."

I sidled up to the kitchen counter and rested my chin on the palms of my hand. She considered me for a few moments before asking, "What is it, *mija*? Did something happen outside?"

I sighed. "I guess you can see it in my face?"

"And sense it too." She set her spoon down and gave me her full attention. "Did that *malo* upset you? Leaf?"

"You think he's *malo*?" I sat up. "Like, a bad guy?"

She rubbed her forehead. "I don't really know. I probably should not call him that, but I can't pinpoint his true intentions. He is heavily clouded with emotions, and I can't see his truth. It bothers me."

"He bothers me too," I said, chipping away at my nail polish. "He said I'm useless and that I don't know anything."

She furrowed her brows, wagging her finger, then mumbled some choice words in Spanish. I couldn't help but laugh.

"*¡Abuela!*"

"*¡Es la verdad!*"

She had a point. But so did Leaf. He had called me out, and rightfully so. "Leaf's not exactly wrong." My voice grew small with shame and guilt. "I should know more about what my mom and dad went through in Faevenly. I should know more about my fae heritage."

She nodded and patted my hand. "It is okay. You are living your life, and all those things that happened in the past are in the past. The story of your *mamá y papá* is their story, not your story. You should not feel bad at all for looking forward at life and not behind. No one could have known there would be new troubles stirring in the fae realm. As for understanding your heritage, there is time for that."

I knew she was right, but I still felt awful about it. Leaf had really hit a nerve. "I guess."

"I should know more about your mother too," she confessed. "But when your father returned with her from Faevenly, he did not want to talk much about what had happened. Neither did your Uncle Manny." She closed her eyes and placed her hand over her heart. "It was all too painful," she said in a low voice.

"It was?" I matched her tone, more guilt building up inside of me. "I didn't know."

She moved her hand to mine and squeezed. "I never pushed them to tell me what they had been through, and the years have passed. And they passed quickly. Now we are here."

Hearing her say that made me feel better. But I was still so agitated about Leaf and the way he looked at me and what he had said.

"But *mija*, I can help you with your Hispanic heritage. You have many gifts passed down through your bloodline as an Avila and a Rodriguez. Gifts that have served your father, myself, and many of our family members well."

"Seeing spirits and having bad vibes?" I asked. "I'm not so sure those serve me well at all."

She chuckled. "Your father thought the same thing. But during the most dire circumstances, he was able to tap into the powers deep within him and call forth his aura like a shield and a weapon. It helped them in Faevenly."

"Really?" When I was little, Dad used to talk about using the light from within him for protection. He said I'd be able to do it when I grew older. But then, for some reason, he stopped talking about it. And I stopped asking. Now it all felt too late.

"Can you show me, *Abuela*? Show me how to use my aura?"

"I do not have that talent, so your father will have to show you. But I can tell you that the light will come forth naturally when you need it."

"Naturally," I muttered, disappointed that she couldn't show me.

"But *mija*, I can help you with the skills I share with your father—the ability to connect your mind and your spirit to others."

Perking up, I thought a skill like that could really help me. "You can?"

"Yes, I can."

"Oh, thank you, *Abuela*!" I hopped off of my stool, feeling rejuvenated and filled with purpose. "Can we do it now?"

"It will take time and practice, but yes." She laughed. "We can start now."

Abuela moved from the stove to the kitchen table and I joined her excitedly. She motioned at a chair across from her, and I slid in.

"When I am working with a client, I always have them sitting in front of me," she explained. She moved the bowl of apples to the counter. "I also clear the table unless I'm using my cards or my crystals. Those things can stay."

I hadn't seen her work in years and didn't understand it at all, so this perspective on what she could do riveted me. Especially since I knew how powerful she was.

She brought her hand up to her chest and patted the cross that hung underneath her shirt. "I touch my cross before each session, and I say a prayer to God for guidance and wisdom. And I ask all the angels and saints to be with me."

Instinctively, my fingers found the cross beneath my shirt. We were Catholic, like most of my family, and I'd gone through all the CCE religious classes. I hadn't expected to like them, but somewhere along the way, I did. Faith fascinated me—the mystery of it, the order, the light. Even with a fae mother from another realm, I still believed in one ultimate power guiding everyone and everything, no matter where they came from.

"Now," she said in a low tone, regarding me with seriousness. "I am going to think of a place, and I want you to clear your mind and see it within me."

"See it within you?" I asked, pulling my chin in. "How do you mean?"

"Yes, see it," she said matter-of-factly. "Just connect with me, *mija*. Let it flow naturally. Like your mind is friends with my mind and they are having a conversation."

"Friends?" I stopped a laugh from escaping my lips. "*Abuela*, really? Is that how you do it?"

She shrugged. "It is the easiest way for me to explain it. But yes. It's a connection. Now come on." She tapped the wood table. "The *caldo* will be ready soon."

"All right. Friends. With your mind. I can do that." I shifted in my seat, then quieted down. I let my shoulders fall. I relaxed my arms and released the tension in my hands.

"Make sure your feet are flat on the ground," she instructed.

"They are," I answered, burrowing my toes into the fluffy rug.

"Very good. Now, clear your mind and then focus on me." She paused for a moment then added, "tell me what I am thinking of."

Closing my eyes and focusing on my mind, a barrage of thoughts hit me—infuriating yet incredibly sexy Leaf, the deadly fae vampire, my parents in Faevenly, my stupid calculus test, and even my chipped nails.

"Try harder," she said. "I sense the clutter."

"Okay," I mumbled. I pushed every random thought away with a silent grunt, creating the blankest slate possible. When my mind was clear enough, I focused on my *abuela*.

A warm tickle filled my belly as feelings of comfort flowed over me—a sip of soothing mint tea, a warm tortilla, a soft blanket. Suddenly, I felt as if I was in

Abuela's home, sitting on her couch. I could almost see the antique dark furnishings and the soothing beige walls. Could practically smell the herbs and spices that always swirled in the air.

Tingles of excitement raced down my body as my eyes flung open. "You're thinking of your living room!"

She smiled big and nodded. "I am. Very good work!"

With my mouth still hanging open, I uttered, "I can't believe I did that."

She went to her pot of soup and lifted the lid to inspect the contents. "I can. You are an Avila, after all."

Abuela was right. I was an Avila, and I should embrace that side of myself. I should step into every part of being a *bruja* and claim my power. I was dumb not to. "Can we do another one?"

"Yes, but not now. This was your first time, so you should rest your mind. Also, the soup is ready."

My mouth watered and my stomach grumbled, but then *Abuela* eyed the door. "You should let Leaf know."

"Are you serious?" I rolled my eyes. "He doesn't deserve your food, not after the way he talked to me."

She furrowed her brows. "It's not right, *mija*. Please don't be rude. We are not like that."

"We are not the rude ones. He is," I huffed.

She kept her stare on me, giving me a look. "*Mija, por favor.*"

Clearly, she was not settling for a no. "Fine," I said, taking my jacket off the hook by the back door and going outside.

Darkness had taken over the sky, the clouds so thick they erased the stars and the moon. I scanned the perimeter of our yard by the glow of our soft landscape lighting, but didn't see Leaf anywhere. Instead of calling out for him like I did before, I thought I'd walk around and see where he was. And I'd start with the area he had come from earlier, near the lake.

With my arms wrapped around my body, I made my way across the grass and to the wooden dock. I peered about, searching for the tall slender fae, but he was nowhere in sight.

"Gabriela?"

I spun around, my hand flying to my chest—then exhaled when I saw Leaf. "Jeez, don't do that! You scared the hell out of me!"

"My apologies. I did not mean to startle you." He eyed my bare feet. "You should not be out here."

"I came to tell you my grandmother made some soup and she's invited you to join us if you want."

He hesitated, as if unsure whether to take me up on my offer, but his hunger must've convinced him to say yes. "Thank you."

"Don't thank me, thank her," I said, leading the way back to the house. Halfway to the door, I stopped and turned around. "And by the way, don't ever call me useless again. And just so you know, not that it's any business of yours, even though I haven't been to Faevenly in a while, it's still very important to me. Okay?"

He studied me for a few seconds. "I did not mean to offend you."

I had no idea if that was an apology or not, but I accepted his answer with a nod and continued on to the house.

Leaf set his weapons near the back door while *Abuela* slipped into her favorite role as hostess. She ushered us toward the stove, where she'd laid out bowls, spoons, and napkins, along with toppings of cilantro, jalapeño, tomato, and onion. She served Leaf first, then me, and filled her own bowl last.

For a moment, life almost felt normal again—like the world beyond the kitchen walls didn't exist. But as we sat at the table, an uncomfortable silence settled over us, heavy and unspoken.

"So, Leaf," *Abuela* said, passing him a plate of piping hot corn tortillas. "Tell us about yourself."

"There is not much to tell," he said, taking a bite of his soup and assuming a tight-lipped demeanor.

"I see," she nodded, taking her own bite. She threw me a look, as if prompting me to say something. I had no interest in chatting, so I gave her a slight shrug and tried not to slurp the soup.

We ate quietly. The clink of spoons against bowls filled the air, but no one spoke. I could feel Leaf's presence like static—alert, careful, as if he didn't quite know what to do with himself. *Abuela* kept her gaze low, every movement precise and polite. I tried to focus on the soup, but the mood had practically ruined the taste.

When he finished, Leaf stood from the table. "Thank you very much for the meal." He lifted his bowl. "May I place this dish somewhere?"

"No, I can do that," *Abuela* said, waving him to leave it alone.

He set the bowl back on the table. With a final nod, he gathered his things and went back outside.

Scooting away from the table, I blew out a long breath. "That was the most awkward meal ever."

"Very," *Abuela* agreed, stacking the dishes and setting them in the sink.

I grabbed a cloth and began wiping the table. "Did you sense anything from him while we ate?"

She shook her head. "Only the same—so many emotions, but nothing specific."

I wanted to find comfort in her words, but the silence he left behind felt heavier than before.

Every instinct in me pointed to him.

About an hour after we'd cleaned the kitchen, *Abuela* went to bed. I got ready too, though I wasn't tired at all. Fresh fear from earlier crept back in. Despite how completely irritating he was, I suddenly felt like Leaf was too far away. And if a fae vampire exploded into the house right now, would he reach me in time? Or my *abuela*?

Not wanting to be weaponless, I slipped out of bed and made my way downstairs. I hesitated by the front door, listening. The house was silent. I retrieved the fighting stick and was about to head back to my room when a thought stopped me. A protector should stay close to the one he's sworn to protect. *Right?*

I crossed to the kitchen and peered through the glass of the back door before stepping outside. The night air was cool against my skin. Without venturing too far, I called softly, "Leaf?"

Within seconds, he appeared from the shadows, his brow quirking as his gaze flicked to the stick in my hands. "Yes?"

"Um, if you don't mind, could you keep your watch from inside? I'd feel a lot safer that way."

"If that is what you wish," he answered formally.

"Yes," I raised my chin. "It's what I wish."

I led him inside and locked the door. His gaze swept the kitchen. "Where would you like me to station?"

We had two large couches in the living room. I could crash on one, and if he needed to lie down, he could take the other. "The living room," I said. "Over here."

The wide-open white-walled room with cream-colored trim had a huge fireplace with a chunky wood mantel and floor-to-ceiling windows. I pointed at the white couches. "I can take one couch and you can take the other."

"I will be standing," he said.

"Oh, okay," I said, not even knowing how he would

stand all night, but chalking it up to a fae protector thing. "Whatever you prefer."

I turned off the lights except for a small lamp in the corner. Leaf took his place by the windows, feet wide and hands behind his back like before. I slipped the blue blanket off the ottoman and draped it over myself, turning away from him as I snuggled into the cushions.

But sleep didn't come easily.

Visions of the soul vamp cluttered my mind as I envisioned his dark eyes, his pointed teeth, the hiss of his voice. I could practically feel his cold breath on my cheek, and could almost hear him calling me a foolish daughter of Strong Haven. His hands were on my throat as he brought his lips up to my mouth.

I sat up with a start, my breathing ragged and shallow, my heart racing out of control.

"Gabriela?" Leaf came over to me and sat beside me on the couch. He tilted his head and placed his hand on my shoulder. "Are you well?"

I rubbed my forehead and shook my head. "I was thinking of that soul vamp and then, suddenly, he was in my mind. Or, I was dreaming. I don't really know."

He touched my shoulder. "I assure you, you are safe. Nothing will harm you while I am here."

I looked into his eyes, wondering how he could be a jerk one moment and kind the next, but grateful for the change. "You're really confusing."

He shifted away, as if afraid to be too close. "I have been through much during these troubling times," he said quietly. "I apologize if my manner is sometimes abrupt."

I leaned in slightly, drawn to the raw emotion in his voice. "What kinds of things?"

He opened and closed his hand. "Things that do not deserve to be spoken of. And if you know what is good for you, you will not ask me again."

He eased back to his post by the windows, shadows tracing the sharp lines of his face. And while I lay there struggling to fall asleep, my thoughts kept circling his words—wondering what he had done, yet afraid to know the truth.

CHAPTER 7

I woke up to bright sunshine streaming through the living room windows. With a yawn, I sat up and looked for Leaf, but he was gone, though I could hear *Abuela* not far in the kitchen. She was playing her favorite Tejano music and, by the smell of it, frying up some bacon.

I got up, went to the restroom, and then joined her.

"*Mija, buenos días.* Why were you on the couch?" She placed the finished bacon on a towel, then started whipping up some scrambled eggs.

"I thought I'd sleep better there. I even asked Leaf to stay in the room with me. I guess I was more freaked out about the soul vamp than I thought."

She nodded. "I understand. It was a good idea." Finishing with the eggs, she set the pan aside and started warming tortillas on the stove. "Breakfast is almost ready. Why don't you get him? He went out the back door when I came downstairs."

Before I could move, my gut clenched. My skin prickled, and the tingle at the back of my neck sharpened into a pulse. I froze. *Abuela* did too. For a long, breathless second, we just stared at each other.

"What's happening?" I whispered, afraid that speaking too loudly might break something fragile in the air.

Her eyes darted around the kitchen, searching for something unseen. "*No sé*," she breathed, fear shadowing her face. "But I feel it too."

The back door flung open and Leaf raced in. He held his bow and arrow at the ready. He whipped it around, searching for a threat. "Who is in here?"

What? Was someone in the room with us? Someone we couldn't see? Scanning for a weapon of my own, I spotted an umbrella by the door. I grabbed it, thinking it was the worst weapon ever, but needing something I could use to defend myself. *Abuela* held out her spatula.

"Show yourself!" Leaf demanded.

An orb illuminated the room, and I recognized it right away. It was a shimmery portal like the one my parents used to cross between the realms. Was it them? Were they coming back? The glow lengthened and stretched out, like a magical curtain being pulled apart until it was the size of a door.

Lady Sonia, the Strong Haven palace healer, came into view. Her long dark hair hung in disarray, and her yellow dress was ripped and shredded at the bottom. She motioned for us to cross over, her gestures quick and desperate.

I whipped my stare over to *Abuela,* icy fear tingling all over. "Something happened to Mom and Dad."

She clutched her shirt where her cross hung, her

eyes revealing deep fear. "Not again," she whispered. "*Por favor, no otra vez.*"

Leaf lowered his bow and arrow. "We must go. They need us."

I knew he was right, but terror held me in place. What was happening in Faevenly?

"Go," *Abuela* said desperately, her strong and warm hands clutching my arm. "Help your *mamá y papá.*"

Her plea jolted me from my fear and doubt, and I hugged her tight. "I promise I'll come back soon."

She nodded with confidence. "Of course you will. Now go, and be careful."

I wanted to tell her I loved her, but thought it would sound like some sort of final goodbye. As if I were leaving forever and wouldn't see her again. Besides, she knew how much I loved her, and I knew how much she loved me. So I held my tongue and turned to Leaf.

"Let's go," I said.

He motioned me to the portal. Even though I hadn't used one in a long time, I remembered exactly what to do. Step through, brace for the weightlessness, then land on solid ground.

Please, let my parents be okay. I took one last look at my *abuela,* held my breath, and then stepped through the warm vapor.

There was no going back now.

With my feet firmly planted on Faevenly soil and Leaf beside me, Lady Sonia quickly placed her hands along the edges of the shimmer, collapsing it until it was small enough to fit in her palm. Then she turned to me.

"My lady Gabriela," she said with a quick bow. "Thank you so much for coming."

I wasn't sure how to respond. I hadn't seen her in such a long time, plus I was completely freaked out. So I offered her a nod. "Of course," I said. "What's going on?"

We were in the garden in the back of the palace surrounded by bright flowering bushes and tall green-leafed trees. Butterflies flitted across my line of sight, and if not for Lady Sonia's disheveled appearance, I would have never known something was up.

"Where are my parents?" I asked.

"And Lord Letormis," Leaf demanded.

He slung his bow across his back and sheathed his arrow in its quiver. He scanned the area with laser-like focus. I lowered my umbrella and scanned the area too. No one was around. Then I noticed I was in my pajama pants and a t-shirt, with no shoes.

"Matters are most dire," Lady Sonia said, her hands trembling. "The palace was stormed not an hour ago. Lord Letormis is injured. Many have been killed."

My heart caught in my throat. "And my mom and dad?" I asked, my voice breaking into panic.

Lady Sonia clasped my hands in hers. "My lady Gabriela, they are not among the dead. But they are also nowhere to be found. I fear they may have been taken."

Leaf's eyes blazed. "By whom?"

Her gaze glossed with tears. "We do not know. Our attackers crept in unseen, picking off the guards one by one. When they entered the palace, a skirmish broke out. The halls echoed with the clash of weapons as I gathered as many servants as I could and hid with them in the tunnel beneath the kitchen. When the noise finally ceased, we emerged." Her expression went distant, her voice a fragile whisper. "Many lost their lives."

My mind spun with horror—every terrible possibility flashing before me. My parents, captured...hurt... worse. My emotions must have been written all over my face, because Leaf placed a steadying hand on my shoulder.

"They are not among the dead, Gabriela." He stepped closer, close enough for me to see the fine stitching on his shirt. His voice dropped low, sharp with conviction. "Gone does not mean dead."

I swallowed hard and forced a nod, fighting back tears. They had to be alive. They just had to be.

"Where is Lord Letormis?" Leaf asked, turning toward Lady Sonia.

"He is in his bedchamber. I've given him a serum made from the healing water of Green Falls. It will take time, but he will recover."

"Very well," Leaf said, a hint of relief in his voice. "Let us go to him at once."

But Lady Sonia didn't move. Something in her face told me there was more.

"What is it?" I asked.

Her bottom lip trembled. "Lady Pen has perished."

Fresh tears blurred my vision, my throat tightening painfully. My dumb life in the human realm—all the useless things I'd thought mattered—had kept me from this place. Now Uncle Leto was hurt, Aunt Pen was dead, and my parents were missing.

Guilt surged through me like a tidal wave.

"My Aunt Pen?" I finally managed to choke out. "She's dead?"

"Yes, Lady Gabriela." Lady Sonia's voice broke, then steadied with effort. "And there is one more horrible thing you both must know."

I couldn't imagine what could be worse, but the terror in her eyes told me it was.

"What is it?" Leaf asked.

"Draven the witch has escaped."

The name hit me like ice. *Draven.* The witch my parents had feared most was free. Which meant this wasn't over. It was only beginning. And in that instant, I knew nothing in any realm would ever be the same.

CHAPTER 8

Everything froze. Time stood still as fear surged through me, tingling panic racing across my skin. Leaf had said Draven was evil, power-hungry, devious, and relentless in his thirst for revenge. Now he was loose.

"Thunderation," Leaf muttered. He turned away, hands curling into fists, and then drove one into the nearest tree.

His reaction startled me, but it told me everything I needed to know. If Draven had escaped, we were doomed.

"He's the one who took my parents, isn't he?" My voice trembled as my body shook uncontrollably. If he had them, we didn't have time.

"We do not know for certain," Lady Sonia said softly, "but I am sorry to say we suspect the same. Lord Letormis has a team searching the dungeons and grounds for any sign of how Draven escaped, or where he might have gone. They are also searching for Lady Celyse and Lord Julio."

My heart pounded out of control. The air felt too thin, the world tilting beneath me as the truth sank in.

Everything I'd known—my home, my family—was slipping away. "What do we do now?"

Leaf stood motionless for a moment, then said, "We must see Lord Letormis. Straight away."

With a sharp nod, Lady Sonia led us toward the palace. As we stepped inside, the brutality of the attack revealed itself. Blood and grime streaked the once-pristine marble floors. Elegant tapestries hung in tatters. Crimson spatter marred the paintings. This wasn't a warning. This was what happened when you were too late.

At the base of the grand staircase, servants and guards tended to the wounded. Farther down the hall lay rows of bodies beneath white sheets. I forced my eyes to the ground, focusing on my feet instead of the carnage. If I looked, it would be real.

"I need shoes," I whispered, my stomach twisting at the thought of walking barefoot through it all.

"Of course, my lady," Lady Sonia said gently. "When we get upstairs, I will see to it."

We dodged the debris, climbed the stairs, and walked the long corridor to the chamber my uncle and aunt shared. The massive door loomed before us— carved with vines and blossoms so lifelike. I used to spend hours tracing them with my fingers as a child, imagining the stories they told. Mom said she used to do the same.

Now she was gone.

Lady Sonia must have sensed my thoughts because

she gave me a faint, reassuring smile before opening the door.

Inside, I expected gloom. Instead, sunlight streamed through open windows, stirring the curtains. Servants surrounded the bed where my uncle sat propped against a mound of pillows, his eyes closed, a white cloth across his forehead.

"Uncle Leto," I rushed to his side as he opened his eyes. "You're okay," I muttered, picturing him to look much worse.

He smiled faintly. "I have been better," he said, "but I have also been worse."

He extended his hand, and I took it gently, afraid of causing pain. I wanted to ask about my parents, but words caught in my throat. "Are you hurt?"

"I was," he admitted. "But thanks to Lady Sonia and the healing waters of the Green Falls, I will recover."

A basin beside the bed held his blood-soaked clothes. I shivered at the thought of what he'd looked like when they brought him in.

He met my gaze, his violet eyes softening. "You know about your parents... and about Pen."

Fresh tears welled in my eyes and I pressed my face into his gown. I should have been here. "Yes," I whispered.

He wrapped his arms around me. "My dear sweet girl," he murmured. "Everything will be all right."

"No, it won't." I pulled back, the pain sharp in my chest. "And don't tell me about the sun and the moon and the stars making everything better, because that's a bunch of crap."

Gasps rose from the corner where the servants stood, but I didn't care. He needed to know what I thought.

Uncle Leto smiled softly. "You never were one to mince words, were you?"

"It's not fair, Uncle. And you know it."

He brushed away my tears. "Life and death are never fair. But I assure you, the losses we suffered today will not go unanswered."

"So there's a plan?" Leaf asked from behind me.

Uncle Leto's gaze shifted. "There will be."

He had the room cleared until only Lady Sonia, Leaf, and I remained. With help, he stood and crossed to a chair near the window.

"What happened here?" Leaf asked, his jaw tight.

"We were attacked, as you saw. By whom, we cannot say. A few have been captured, but they are not talking. Not yet, anyway. But Draven was most assuredly behind it." He winced, pressing a hand to his chest.

"And my parents?" I asked. "What happened to them?"

His face softened with sorrow. "They were either taken by Draven—or escaped and await their moment to return. I am sorry, Gabriela. I should have protected them better."

I squeezed his hand. "This isn't your fault, Uncle. You'd never put them in danger. I know that."

We sat in silence for a moment before Leaf spoke again, voice low and heavy. "And Draven? How did he get out of the dungeon?"

"I do not know," Uncle Leto said grimly. "A team is investigating. I can only hope they find answers."

Leaf began to pace, anger simmering beneath his calm. "This is all my fault. If I'd been here, I could have stopped it."

My stomach twisted. Had this happened because Leaf was guarding me instead? Was this my fault too? I swallowed hard, pushing the thought away. I couldn't afford to break. Not now. I was my parents' daughter—Strong blood and human magic both—and I had to help however I could.

"No, Leaf," Uncle Leto said firmly. "If Draven was meant to escape, he would have. You being here would have changed nothing."

"Perhaps." Leaf's jaw tightened. "But it is no matter now. He will come for Lady Gabriela next. If I am to protect her, I need to get her into hiding."

I froze. "Is that true?" I asked my uncle. "Is he coming for me?"

Uncle Leto crossed his arms but didn't answer. Instead, he turned to Lady Sonia. "Do you sense anything?"

She closed her eyes and held her hands together in front of her. "I do not sense that he is near—or that he is coming. Not yet, anyway."

Uncle Leto nodded and turned to me. "And you, Lady Gabriela? Do you sense anything?"

"Me?" I blinked, pointing at myself as if he could've meant someone else.

"Yes," he said. "You are the daughter of a fae princess and a human witch. Power runs in your veins. It is time you learned to use it."

My heart lurched and my pulse jumped. "I'm...not really equipped for that."

"Nonsense!" He stood abruptly, surprising me with his strength. "You are equipped, girl! Your gifts are within you!"

I stepped back, overwhelmed. My aunt was dead. My uncle wounded. My parents missing. And now a fae witch was hunting me next. And my uncle wanted me to *sense things?* I didn't even know how to begin.

"I told you," Leaf muttered. "She cannot do anything."

That did it. I spun on him. "I don't know what I did to make you hate me, but you need to back off. Got it?"

He didn't flinch. "Got it," he said flatly.

Before I could say more, Lady Sonia intervened with a calm smile. "As I sense no immediate threat, allow me to take Lady Gabriela for a wash and fresh garments."

Uncle Leto sank back into his chair. "If it is fine with Lady Gabriela, it is fine with me."

"It's fine," I said quickly, desperate to escape the heaviness in the room. I also really needed to get out of my pajamas.

Lady Sonia held out her hand. "Shall I take your umbrella?"

I paused, not realizing I was still clutching it. "Sure."

She took it gently and motioned toward the door. Before I followed, I glanced back at Uncle Leto. "What will happen to Aunt Pen and the others?"

"They will be prepared for the Passing Place," he said quietly. "We will see to it in the morning."

I crossed the room and wrapped my arms around Uncle Leto, careful of his injuries. For a moment, he held me like he used to when I was small, and I let myself breathe. Then I followed Lady Sonia out, clutching what little courage I had left.

CHAPTER 9

Walking out of the room with Lady Sonia, my mind drifted to what it meant to go to the Passing Place. My parents had never described a fae funeral, but my imagination filled in the blanks— being sent out to sea on a small boat, or set upon a pyre of wood and flame. Or maybe, somehow drifting into the sky like that cat from that musical. As a daughter of a fae princess, I really should've known this stuff.

"Lady Gabriela?" Lady Sonia's voice pulled me from my morbid thoughts.

"Oh, sorry," I shook my head a little. "Were you talking to me?"

She smiled faintly, her expression softening. "I was asking if you were all right, my lady."

I hesitated, unsure how to answer. How could I be all right when my aunt was dead, my uncle wounded, and my parents were missing? Not to mention a vindictive fae vampire witch was on the loose. "I don't know," I admitted quietly. "I think I'm still trying to understand how everything fell apart so fast."

Lady Sonia nodded, her gaze distant but kind.

"Grief has a way of bending time. It can make every moment feel too long and too short all at once."

Her words settled deep inside me, a mix of comfort and truth that only made my chest ache more. Regret bubbled to the surface.

"I'm sorry I stopped visiting." The words felt wholly inadequate, but they were all I had. I started to explain how busy I'd been, then stopped. My excuses meant nothing. I hadn't made the effort to learn about Faevenly or the part of me that belonged here. I'd chosen not to. And now, standing in the middle of all this loss, I had no one to blame but myself.

Sonia patted my arm. "Please, my lady. Do not do that to yourself." Her touch was gentle but firm, the way my mother's was when she wanted to quiet my racing thoughts. "There is no blame to carry. You are here now, and that is what matters. The past cannot be changed, but what you do next—that is where your power lies."

Power? What power? Her words were kind, yet they cut deep because I was powerless. I desperately wanted to believe her, to let that guilt slip away, but it clung to me all the same.

She led me down the hall and to the wing where my mother's childhood bedroom was. Further down the hall was her sister Malena's room. Malena had died years ago, before I was born, so I didn't know much about her. Which was yet another part of all the stuff I hadn't bothered asking about.

Beyond the bedrooms were a library, a study, and a huge washroom, where Lady Sonia now paused, her hand on the doorknob. "While you are tended to, I will search for a dress and some shoes for you."

"A dress?" My mother was a princess, and that technically made me one too, but I wasn't too fond of dresses and only wore them when I had to. "Can I get pants instead?"

"Of course, my lady, whatever pleases you," she said with a nod. She motioned to the door. "Maid Gidna awaits you, and I shall return shortly."

Maid Gidna rushed toward me the instant I stepped into the vast washroom. She was a stocky dwarf with short-cropped red hair and a face full of freckles. She threw her arms around me and squeezed, her grip so strong and tight a grunt pushed through my lips.

"My lady Gabriela, it has been too long!" she exclaimed in her unusually soft voice, one that never quite matched her sturdy frame. I hugged her back, sinking into the warmth of her embrace, breathing in the scent of honey and soap. And that was the moment my tears came.

They slipped free before I could stop them, hot and relentless. I tried to speak—tried to say *I'm sorry*, or *I missed you*, or even just *thank you*—but the words caught somewhere between my heart and my throat. All I could do was hold on tighter as the weight of everything crashed over me.

"My dear. My sweet dear." She pulled back just enough to look at me, using the towel draped over her arm to dab at my face. "Everything will work itself out. As sure as the sun rises and falls, this season will pass, and a better one will come. I am sure of it."

Unable to hold it in any longer, the guilt spilled out of me. "Oh, Gidna, I should've visited more. I should've spent more time with Aunt Pen. I should've learned more about this realm. I should've—" my voice broke "—done a lot of things."

"Now, now. There is no sense in should-haves. Do you hear me? None at all." She hugged me again, rocking me from side to side, patting my back as if I were a child. And in that moment, I felt like one—sad, vulnerable, and scared.

Finally, my tears subsided, and my shoulders stopped shaking. I pulled back. "I want to believe that, I really do, but I just don't know."

"You need to trust, that is all." She stroked my cheeks. "And take a soothing bath. It will help, my dear lady."

"Okay," I nodded. " Thank you, Gidna."

The washroom gleamed and sparkled from all the white marble and flecks of gold. In the middle of the room sat a huge tub, almost like a small pool. It was filled to the brim with pink-colored water with crimson and lavender petals sprinkled on the top. A trio of tiny maid servants with short-cropped brown hair adorned with decorative twigs and leaves were near the edge of the tub, tending to the water and adding powders and herbs.

Maid Gidna guided me to a small bench. "Would you like us to undress you, or would you prefer to do that yourself?"

"I can do it."

"Very well, my dear." Her tone was gentle, practical. "And your necklace and earrings, shall I take them, or would you rather leave them on?"

"On, please." The words came faster than I meant them to. I couldn't bear to be parted from them. My parents had given them to me years ago, and I almost never took them off.

"Very good," she said, inclining her head. "We will give you some privacy. We won't be far if you should need us."

"Thank you, Gidna."

She squeezed my shoulder before she left, a small gesture that somehow said everything words couldn't.

After the room emptied, I stripped off my clothes, then eased myself into the tub. The warm water instantly melted away my tension, then soothed me, caressing my body like tiny little waves of acupuncture. The sweet scent of the flowers relaxed my mind. I had no idea what they had put in the water, but it felt amazing.

After a few minutes, I lowered myself into the water, sinking down to the bottom. I stayed there and watched the tiny bubbles escape my mouth. With my lungs near bursting, I rose to the surface. And there, alone and surrounded by the comforting liquid, I cried again. I let every last tear drop from my eyes, because I didn't know what I would do if I lost my mom and dad.

When my tears were emptied and my hands had started to prune, I climbed out of the tub and wrapped myself with the large towel that had been left for me.

A soft knock sounded before the door creaked open. "All finished, my lady?" Gidna's voice floated in, light and warm. She must have heard the splash of water.

"Yes, I'm finished," I said, glad to have her back.

She entered with the other maidservants, carrying a robe of pale cream and a pair of soft slippers. "Here we are," she said, smiling as she helped me into the robe. The fabric was thick and impossibly soft, like being wrapped in a cloud.

With the robe on, Gidna ushered me to a plush chair positioned before a large, ornate mirror framed in curling gold vines. "Sit, my dear," she said, patting the seat. "Let us make you feel yourself again."

Gidna and another maid servant worked on my hands, using thin nail files. They scrubbed away my chipped nail polish and then shaped my fingernails. When they finished, they sprayed my hands and arms with oil and started rubbing.

With that finished, Gidna took out a shaved shell, like a skinny comb, then worked it through my strands of long, wet hair.

"I had forgotten how you use shells as combs," I said.

Maid Gidna glanced at it. "What do you use to groom your hair in the human realm?"

"A brush that's wooden, or plastic, that has bristles."

She raised a brow. "What is plastic?"

"Well..." I searched for a way to describe the material. "Plastic is a hard material that's made in a factory."

She wrinkled her nose and made a face. "That sounds dreadful."

"That's because it *is* dreadful," I admitted, heat rising to my cheeks. A flicker of shame stirred in me for my realm and all its pollution and waste.

Before Gidna could ask anything else, the door swung open and in walked Lady Sonia. She had cleaned up and changed out of her dirtied yellow dress into a long, elegant gray one. In her arms, she carried a neatly folded stack of clothes.

"I have a tunic, trousers, and a pair of slippers for the princess," she said with a slight tip of her head.

Maid Gidna's eyes went wide as she glanced from Lady Sonia to me. "Working clothes for the princess? Not a dress?"

"I didn't want a dress, Gidna," I said simply.

Her stunned expression lingered a moment longer before softening into acceptance. "If that is what you wish," she said at last, giving a small shrug.

Lady Sonia turned to leave, but I stopped her. "Wait," I said, rising from the chair. "Before you go...

could I use your shimmer portal? I'd like to speak with my *abuela*. I need to let her know I'm okay and tell her what's happening."

Shimmers were connected to either people or places. Sometimes both. And Lady Sonia's was obviously connected to my house. I wondered how many times she, or others, had visited my mom and dad and I hadn't known.

"Of course, my lady," she said. Reaching into the pocket of her gown, she drew out the small shimmer. Shaped so small like that, it reminded me of a translucent cotton ball. She held it out to me and set it on the palm of my hand. "Do you remember how to use it?"

It had been a long time since I'd used a shimmer, but my parents had taught me when I was little. I was pretty sure it was like riding a bike. "I do."

"Good. Take your time," she said gently. She turned to the others. "Come, let us give the princess her privacy."

At her command, Gidna and the maidservants bowed and filed out quietly, the soft sweep of their skirts fading from the washroom. When the door closed, the room felt larger, quieter—almost sacred.

Placing the shimmer on the bench, I quickly removed the robe and slipped on the clothing Sonia had brought me. The crisp white shirt hugged my body just right, almost as if it was tailor-made just for me. And the forest green pants with the intricate stitching on the sides slid on with ease. A thick brown belt finished the look.

Now that I was dressed, and with the calming effects of the bath working on me, it was time to see my *abuela*.

Scooping up the shimmer, I brought my palm up to my face and studied it. Warmth emanated from the small object, like a campfire glow. Yet the heat didn't bother my skin at all. I carefully placed my fingers on the edges, then stretched it out slowly. The peephole-sized view of my kitchen grew until I could see the entire space.

My *abuela* dashed into view. "*¡Mija!*" she mouthed.

With the opening as big as a doorway, I stepped through, coming to a stop in front of her. She rushed me with a hug. "*Mija,*" she uttered between sobs. "*¡Dios mío!* I have been so worried!"

My eyes watered over, and a fresh tears spilled out onto my cheeks. "I'm so sorry, *Abuela*. I should've come to you sooner."

She pulled back and waved away my apology, then wiped away my tears with her hands. "It's okay. You're here now." She glanced over my shoulder at the opening behind me. "*¿Tu mamá y papá?*"

My stomach twisted tight. "*Abuela*... they're missing."

She stumbled back, as if physically punched, her eyes bewildered and confused. "Missing?"

"Yes," I swallowed. "Strong Haven palace was attacked. A lot of fae were killed, including Aunt Pen, and nobody knows where Mom and Dad are."

She walked to the kitchen counter and sat on the

stool, stunned. "Missing," she muttered, making the sign of the cross.

I gave her some time to process, then asked, "Have you been able to sense anything?"

"No," she said with a shake of her head. "I cannot see anything, though I have been trying." She stayed silent, and I could tell her mind was churning. But then her eyes went wide with an idea. She got up and clutched my arms. "But you, you can do it. You must go back and use everything you are as an Avila and a fae to find them."

I had intended to go back and do what I could, but deep inside, I thought Leaf was right—that I was useless. But with *Abuela's* blessing and her belief, along with Uncle Leto's, those limiting thoughts began to fade like fog in sunlight.

"You really think I can? Because I don't know where to start."

"*Absolutamente.* I have no doubt in my mind that you can do it." Her voice was steady, threaded with the kind of conviction that only comes from love. "You come from a long line of fighters, *mija.* It's in your blood to rise when others would fall."

Emotion welled in my throat as I nodded. "I'll do everything I can to find them and bring them home." My voice trembled with a mixture of fear and resolve. "I promise."

Abuela's smile was soft but full of light. "I know you will." She cupped my face in her warm, wrinkled hands. "Remember who you are. You are Gabriela

Sarah Avila. Inside you are great and powerful gifts passed on from your father, from me, and from generations before us. These gifts may be buried deep, but they are there, and they will always help you when you need them. You only need to have faith."

"Faith," I repeated. For the first time since everything had fallen apart, it didn't feel impossible. It felt like a beginning.

"Yes, *mija*. Faith is a warrior." She hugged me and held on tight. I could tell she didn't want to be the first to break the embrace, and neither did I, but eventually she lowered her arms and kissed my cheeks. "Now go, *mija*. God will be with you."

"Thank you, *Abuela*."

For a moment, I just looked at her—the lines around her eyes, the warmth in her smile, the quiet strength that had carried our family through so much. I wanted to memorize every detail, to hold on to it for when the world turned dark again. Because if faith was a warrior, then so was she.

I left her and stepped back into Faevenly, then collapsed the portal and balanced it on my hand, a sense of strength slowly building inside me.

"I'm finished," I called out.

Lady Sonia and Maid Gidna entered the room. Lady Sonia held out her hand, and I passed her the shimmer. She slipped it into her pocket and gave me a reassuring nod.

"Did all go well with your grandmother?" she asked.

"It did," I said, a renewed sense of purpose stirring inside me. I was going to do everything I could to find my parents—and to believe that the gifts buried within me would awaken when I needed them most.

I only prayed that when that time came, they'd be enough.

CHAPTER 10

W hen Lady Sonia and I stepped out of the
washroom, we found Leaf leaning against the
wall, dagger at his belt, bow and quiver behind his
back. He stood erect when he saw me, and gave me and
Lady Sonia a short nod. Lady Sonia returned the
gesture, but I refused to acknowledge him.

"Gabriela," Lady Sonia explained. "Leaf will be
continuing his protection while you are here. But if
you need anything beyond what he can assist you with,
please let me know."

"Where is Uncle Leto?" I asked, preferring to be
with him instead.

"He is taking time for himself today, and I will be
tending to the fallen." She motioned to Leaf. "You will
be in capable hands with Leaf." Then she motioned
back to the closed door of the washroom. "And of
course, Maid Gidna is always at your disposal."

"Of course," I muttered. "Thank you, Lady Sonia."

She left with a nod and a smile, her dress rustling
softly with her footsteps as she made her way down
the corridor and toward the stairs.

I clasped my hands in front of me, not at all thrilled

about being alone with Leaf, but I guess I had no choice. Uncle Leto was busy and the palace staff was consumed with cleaning up after the attack. I wanted to stay out of the way while also making myself useful. But I felt lost, lacking the basic knowledge I needed to lend a hand. If there was any time for me to reconnect with Faevenly, this was it. Reacquainting myself with the palace would be a good start.

"Since we're stuck together, how about showing me around? You've been so great at reminding me how useless I am and how long I've been away. I think walking around my fae home would do me good."

"Of course," he said. "It would be my pleasure. But it would be best to keep to the grounds. The palace is still in disarray."

"The grounds will be fine," I said, not wanting to think about the floors of the palace again.

Before he started walking, he relaxed his stance, dropping his formality. Even the hard edges around his face softened. "I ask your forgiveness for saying you do not know anything. I should not have."

Now *that* was unexpected. No doubt he was forced to apologize. Maybe by Uncle Leto, or Lady Sonia. I thought of replying with some sort of snarky comment, but decided against it. It wouldn't do any good. "It's okay, Leaf."

Staying by my side, he led me down the corridor, away from the main staircase, and to a narrow one toward the rear of the floor we were on. Like my own personal tour guide, he started pointing out things.

"These stairs are mostly used by the staff. If you take them up, you will find yourself in the corridor for the servants. If you take them down, it will lead to the wing where the cook house and healing chamber are."

"That's right," I said, remembering the layout. "I used to climb up and down the stairs all the time when I was little."

He stopped and studied me. "Why did you stop visiting Faevenly?"

Again, I thought of all the excuses I could offer him, but didn't want to. "I've been wondering that myself," I said honestly.

"Hmm," he grunted, considering my reply, yet keeping his thoughts to himself.

He continued on to the narrow stairwell and made his way down to the first floor where we emerged into a small hallway. He pointed to the right. "That way is the cook house." Then he pointed to the left. "Over there is the healing chamber. Where would you like to go?"

My stomach grumbled and I gestured to the right, thinking of how my *abuela* was cooking breakfast when I left. "I could use a bite to eat."

"I could as well," he said, almost acting like a normal person.

A thick aroma of spices and herbs filled my nose as we stepped into the stone cook house. A large wooden table took up the big space in the middle. To the right was a woodfire stove; to the left and the rear were shelves lined with pots, pans, jugs, and jars, along with several cloth-wrapped loaves of bread.

As I stood there, a memory swept me away. "I used to make bread down here with a young meal servant named Lana," I muttered.

"I know whom you speak of," he said, walking across the floor and taking a jug of drink and loaf of bread.

"Is she"—I thought of everyone who had died in the skirmish—"dead?"

"I know not," he answered. "But if it pleases you, I can inquire later."

"I would appreciate that," I said. "Thank you."

He held up the jug and bread. "We can stroll outside with these and I can show you the gardens."

With all the doom and gloom shrouding the palace, and all the death, going outside was a good idea. "That sounds perfect right now."

When we left the palace, the bleakness hanging over me seemed to lift a little. Not a cloud dotted the pure blue sky, and the greenery of the shrubs and trees glistened like glitter. Leaf uncorked the jug and handed it to me. I took a gulp of the drink, and an explosion of fruity freshness slid down my throat. It was the most delicious juice I'd ever had, sweet and tart, but also cool and refreshing. I handed the jug back to him, and he passed me the bread.

"Do you recall Torch Lake, where the shimmers are stored?" he asked.

"Oh, yes. I remember Torch Lake. My mom and I spent many afternoons there when I was little. She'd tell me all about the times she and her childhood friend and guard, Jaid, used to sneak away to the shimmers to watch them floating along the water."

Leaf and I kept walking, passing the jug and bread between us. Not far in the distance sprawled a wooded area. "Torch Lake is beyond those trees. If you would care to see it, we can go that way. It is not far."

"I'd love that," I said.

We wound our way down the gravel path of the manicured garden until eventually the pathway ended and blended in with the natural brush and foliage of the wild.

"The lake is still guarded, so we are safe," he said.

We kept our way and started going through the woods. The trees were tall and skinny, with white bark and colorful leaves of yellow and green. We weren't very deep in when Leaf stopped. He slid his arm around my waist and pulled me behind him. Then he slowly set the jug and the bread on the ground.

"We are not alone," he said in a low voice.

He reached back for his bow and an arrow, nocking it as he kept his eyes sharp. Spotting the black onyx dagger at his belt, I unsheathed it, then turned around so that my back was against his.

"What it is?" I asked, peering about and looking for signs of attackers.

"I do not know." He peered over his shoulder at me, eyeing the dagger. "Do you know how to use that?"

I raised a brow. "Of course."

The back of my neck tingled with alarm as a shrieking trill exploded all around us. My gaze snapped to the sky. Red birds as big as eagles circled high above us. Fire traced the edges of their feathers as their wings thundered through the air. Leaf unleashed an arrow, but they flew too high to hit.

"Holy hell," I said, my heartbeat picking up speed. "What are those things?"

"They are Raróg, or fire demon birds. They live mostly in the area around High Meadow and rarely venture this far east." His eyes narrowed and his nostrils flared. "No doubt they were sent by the Kanes."

The birds screeched, and one by one, they began diving through the trees, coming at us from all sides. Everywhere their wings brushed the branches, leaves caught fire. If we didn't take them out quickly, we'd soon be surrounded by an inferno.

Leaf took aim at the first bird that shot toward us and fired, the arrow slicing clean through its neck. The creature crashed into the underbrush, igniting a fresh blaze as the flames on its wings guttered out. He reloaded swiftly and held his aim as two more burst from the trees ahead of me. He took one down while I kept my sights on the other. When it swooped close, I lunged with my dagger, slicing it across the breast and sending it tumbling. It hit the ground at my feet, and I stomped out the spreading flames before they could catch.

Another circling bird opened its mouth, letting out an ear-piercing screech as it spread its massive wings, coming down at us at breakneck speed.

"Take it out, take it out!" I urged Leaf, my panic rising as the fire spread from tree to tree in the forest.

Leaf held his aim, following the bird as it swung right, then left, then right again. When it got closer, he fired, anticipating the path of the bird with precision. The arrow whisked through the air, driving straight through the bird's head. It plummeted to the ground in a puff of red plumage and sparks.

I spun around, scanning the forest for signs of the last bird, when Leaf yelled, "Look out!"

I ducked as talons tore through my hair, narrowly missing my scalp. I drove the dagger upward on instinct, catching what might've been a foot, but the creature's heat surged over me as it beat its wings and wheeled away for another pass.

"To me, Gabriela!" Leaf hollered.

I moved toward him just as he twisted, swung his bow around, and fired an arrow through the bird's back. With a crack, it crumpled to the ground.

He rushed to stamp out the sparks, then returned to my side. "Are you hurt?"

Threading my fingers through my hair, I searched for injuries but found none. "I'm okay."

Two guards rushed into the clearing from the direction of Torch Lake. "We saw the fire demons," one said. "Are they all down?"

"Yes," Leaf said. He pointed to the flames crackling among the trees. "We need to put the fire out."

"The selkies are already working on it," the second

guard said. "We alerted them and hey are bringing water."

Selkies?

As he spoke, several tall naked women with long dark hair that clung to their pale skin and covered most of their bodies strode our way. They carried what appeared to be... bagpipes? They marched up to the burning trees and squeezed the instruments, which then shot water high up into the treetops, dousing the flames. I stood stunned, watching the selkie fire brigade put out the fires, while Leaf went to retrieve his arrows that hadn't burned up.

He refilled his quiver, slung his bow back into place, then picked up the jug and the bread, which had somehow remained untouched at his feet. His face was hardened with anger and his earlier casual demeanor wiped away as he turned back to me. "We must tell Lord Letormis what has transpired here."

He nodded to the guards and took off in the direction of the palace. Matching his quick pace, my mind spun with questions. But one overrode the others.

"Who are the Kanes?" I asked. "I mean, I know you mentioned them back at my house, but what's their story? Why would they send attack birds like that?"

He stopped and brought his glare down on me. "The Kanes care only for their own power and nothing else. They consorted with Draven and tried to kill your mother and father when they were here many years ago. I was there. I lived it and I fought it. The Kanes also cast out their own children if they are deemed unworthy, throwing them to the wolves like scraps of garbage."

I gulped. "Leaf, I didn't know any of that."

"Of course you did not. You are more human than fae; you do not *know* this place. Nor do you care for its inhabitants or respect its history," he scowled.

He continued on, walking two paces ahead of me, and I wasn't having it. I grabbed his arm and jerked him to a stop, stepping in front of him to make sure I had his attention. "I am over your attitude, okay? I know I haven't been here enough, and I know I don't know as much as I should, but give me a chance!"

He shook his head. "It is too late for that."

I was ready to fire off a nasty response, but something stopped me. Something wounded and heart-wrenching deep in his blue eyes. I reached out and placed my hand on his arm.

"What happened to you? Why are you so mad?"

He placed his hand on mine and kept it there. "It is nothing you would understand."

"Try me."

He gazed deep into my eyes, sending my heart thrumming against my body. For a second there, I thought he might close the gap and kiss me. But instead, he broke the connection and stepped away.

"We must go to Lord Letormis, now."

We walked in silence back to the palace. We made our way through the gardens then into the palace and to Uncle Leto's door as he was walking out.

"Gabriela, Leaf," he eyed us with a raised brow, scanning our harried appearances. "Is all well?"

"No, all is not well," Leaf asserted. "We were attacked by a group of Raróg, no doubt sent by the Kanes."

"Thunderation," Leto spat. He rubbed his forehead and drew in a deep breath. "Are either of you hurt?" He placed his hands on my shoulder and inspected my face.

"I'm fine, Uncle Leto."

"And you?" he asked Leaf.

Leaf gave him a look. "Of course I am fine."

"And the forest? Any fires or other destruction?"

"None. The selkies took care of that," Leaf explained. "And we left the lake guards to tend to the area."

"Good." Leto dropped his hands from my shoulder. "I am needed in the healing chamber to assist Lady Sonia as we make preparations for tomorrow's ceremony. We will have to discuss this later. And whatever you two do, please be careful. I cannot take another catastrophe right now. And neither can Strong Haven."

Leto took quick strides away from us, and once again I was alone with Leaf, feeling completely and utterly confused by him. And once again, I had no idea what to do with myself. With Uncle Leto gone, the preparations being made in the palace for the funeral, and the dangers of the outdoors, I thought I was safest in my room.

"I guess I'm going to my room now," I muttered.

Leaf stayed behind me, as I made my way to my room. When we got there, I wondered if he'd still be the one guarding me. "Will you be the one staying outside my door?"

"I will."

Unsure if I should say okay, or good, or thanks, I settled on a slight nod and went inside my room.

The aroma of roses, gardenias, and lavender floated in the room, instantly calming me. Forcing my thoughts away from Leaf, I scanned the space.

Everything looked the way it did when I was here last. Orbs floated along the shiny ceiling, providing soft light. A large white rug covered most of the floor. Grand wooden furnishings filled the room—a large canopy bed with a bedside table, a desk and a chair, a wardrobe, and a chaise positioned by an open window. A door in the corner led to a private washroom.

Circling the space, I spotted a note and a vial on the desk, along with a spread of cheeses, crackers, fruit, and a pitcher of rose-colored water. I plopped a strawberry in my mouth, savoring the sweetest taste, and read the note.

Lady Gabriela,

In this vial is a calming mixture you might find useful for sleep. Two drops under the tongue should suffice. There is a nightdress in the wardrobe, as well as fresh clothes for the morning.

Lady Sonia

I opened the vial and brought it to my nose, and a strong scent of lavender hit my senses in the most relaxing way. I closed it, then twirled it in my hand. If I took it, I'd probably have an amazing sleep. But what if something happened in the middle of the night and I needed to wake but couldn't? Dangers lurked in Faevenly, and I needed to stay sharp and ready, so I placed the vial back on the desk. Besides, it wasn't even dark yet, though looking outside the large window, I saw the sun was setting.

With nothing for me to do, and with exhaustion slowly taking me over, I went to the washroom to get ready for bed. And when I came out, I found a purple nightgown draped over the foot of the bed. I glanced about, expecting to see Maid Gidna, but didn't. She had either swooped in quickly, or another servant had. Taking off my clothes and slipping on the satin gown, I crawled under the silky smooth sheets, hoping everything would be better in the morning.

The morning brought a somber mood to Strong Haven as everyone prepared for the mass fae funeral. Maid Gidna explained the ceremony as she helped me get ready.

She applied a floral-scented serum on my hair and started combing. "The bodies are prepared with meticulous care. They are washed, oiled, and dressed in the finest white silk."

"Who prepares them?" I asked, envisioning some sort of magical fae funeral parlor.

"Lady Sonia and the other healers. It is part of their service to the palace. Tending to the dead is a great honor." She finished with the comb and started braiding a long lock of hair on one side.

"Where do the bodies go?" I asked.

"To the Passing Place, which is a magical meadow in a mystical unknown region of Faevenly. There, the bodies are returned to nature and transformed into something new." She had finished my hair and started working on my face creams.

"Transformed into something new?" I asked. "Like what?"

"Oh," she mused. "A butterfly, a bird, a blade of grass. Maybe a brand new fae. It all depends on nature and the sun and the moon and the stars."

I raised a brow. "Are you being serious?"

Her mouth fell open. "My lady, I take great offense to that question! There is nothing more sacred than going to the Passing Place."

"Oh my goodness, I didn't mean it that way! I'm so sorry, Gidna. It's just so interesting to me. We do things a lot differently in the human realm."

She closed her mouth, satisfied with my apology, and kept working on my face. "What do you do with the dead in the human realm?"

"Well, we either bury them in the ground or cremate them."

She paused her brushing and shot me a confused look. "What is cremate?"

"It's when the dead are burned, and then the family gets the ashes. It's called cremation."

Her makeup brush tumbled out of her hand as she gasped. "Humans burn their dead?"

"Some, not all." I thought of my great-grandmother's ashes that my *abuela* had in a vase by her bed. "Explaining it makes it sound awful, but it's really not."

She shook her head. "I know the human realm is part of you, and I do not mean to offend, but my dear, cremation sounds quite cruel."

I shrugged. "I don't think so. I'd rather have that done to me then be stuck in the ground."

She tapped my forehead. "Or you can return here and go to the lovely Passing Place when it is your time."

"There's that." The idea of living in Faevenly and being a part of a land where the dead went to the Passing Place actually sounded comforting. As if my heart and soul actually wanted to be here more than the human realm.

When my hair and face were ready, I slipped on a long silver dress, because, as Maid Gidna informed me, everyone wore their best silver to the Passing Place ceremony.

Sparkly crystals lined the gown, and the neckline was a modest scoop. I wondered if Leaf would be wearing silver too. Or if he'd stay in his guard attire. When I stepped out into the hallway, I found out.

His dark hair was pulled back in a long ponytail, and he wore dark silver pants with a white shirt. I almost tripped over myself, he was so striking. But then I remembered how irritating he was.

He held out his hand and gestured toward the stairs. Taking the lead, I made my way to the ground floor and out the entrance to the front garden, where the ceremony would take place.

When I stepped out into the bright sun, I saw the bodies lined up along the gravel road. They were clothed in white silk gowns and lined up in rows. If you didn't know what had happened, you'd think they weren't dead at all, but only sleeping. It was strange and mysterious, and creepy, to see the bodies looking so fresh and peaceful on the ground outside the palace.

Uncle Leto stayed near Aunt Pen's still form, his eyes burdened with sorrow. He knelt beside her, stroking her arm, whispering words to her I couldn't hear. Leaf had left my side and distanced himself from the crowd. Even though he kept his head down, I could see the deep pain in his face. As if sensing my gaze, he raised his head and his stare met mine. I wanted to look away, but it was too late. He held my gaze with intense sorrow for a few long seconds before dropping it and looking back down at the ground.

Murmuring filtered through the crowd, the kind that was sprinkled with sadness and tears. Heads began turning in the direction of the gravel road. I shifted about, trying to see what everyone was looking at, when two magnificent white horses came clopping up to the front of the palace. They towed a large wooden flatbed cart behind them. Nobody rode the horses, and nobody manned the bed of the trailer, either. Gidna hadn't explained this part to me. I must've worn a perplexed look, because Lady Sonia came over.

"Those are Enbarr. They traverse both land and sea, and are swifter than the wind. They will transport the dead to the Passing Place where they will be returned to nature and take on a new life," she whispered in a reverent tone.

The dead... Suddenly, I realized I hadn't seen any

spirits. With the dead all around me, I should've seen one or two by now.

"Lady Sonia, you know how I can see spirits, right? Well, I'm not seeing any right now. Why is that?"

"That is because these dead do not yet know they are dead. They are still inside their bodies."

I blinked. I hadn't heard that before, but I supposed it was possible for a spirit to not yet know their body was no longer alive. Looking at the fae on the ground, I imagined those spirits lingering inside because they thought they were still living.

Golden rays from the morning sun spread across the sky as the bodies of the fallen were lifted one by one and placed on the trailer. Uncle Leto stayed close to Aunt Pen until everyone was loaded. When it was her turn, he scooped her up with care. I rushed over, wanting to be there for him, and for her, and held her small hand that dangled at her side. Uncle Leto smiled with gratitude, then eased her up on the trailer. When she was in place, we backed away, arm in arm. Scanning the faces of the fallen, I spotted Lana, the young maiden I had made bread with so long ago. My sorrow magnified and my heart hurt, and I thought of all the fae in white whose lives had been taken so cruelly.

Lady Sonia started singing a melancholy tune. Others joined in, and soon the Enbarr began their slow trot. The tune faded while the trailer disappeared from view. When it was gone, so was the song.

Uncle Leto sighed. "My dear Gabriela, I must seek solitude this day, if you do not mind."

"No, not at all," I swallowed. "Take whatever time you need."

"Maid Gidna will see that you have everything you need. As for safety, I have asked Leaf to continue his watch indefinitely, and I advise you to stay within the palace property line. If you venture outside, stay away from the woods and the shadows. We have plenty of guards on duty, and the forces around the perimeter of Strong Haven have been doubled. Tomorrow will bring a fresh perspective regarding our predicament, and we can start planning our next move then."

"Sure, Uncle." I gave him a hug. "Don't worry about me, but I have to ask. Is there any word on my parents?"

He let out a somber sigh. "There is no word."

I wasn't standing alone long before Maid Gidna joined me. "My lady, it is a somber day and many will be mourning. I fear the bulk of your day may see you in your bedchamber. I can bring you food and drink and perhaps some books. Maybe some drawing instruments. But first, you must be famished. Can I prepare a spread for you?"

I hadn't eaten yet and wasn't anywhere near being hungry, but thought I should have a little something. "A small spread sounds fine. Thank you, Gidna."

"Of course. Would you prefer to eat in the garden or in your room?"

"My room, please."

She shuffled away and my attention went back to Leaf. He was leaning against a tree with his arms crossed and his head down. I walked over to him and watched for a minute as others around us started filtering back into the palace.

"My uncle says you are still watching over me."

"I am."

When Maid Gidna mentioned many would be in mourning, it became clear that included Leaf. "Did you know any of the dead?"

He kept his gaze on the spot where the bodies had been. "I did. They were all good folk. I see that you saw young Lana among them."

"Yes, I saw her," I said softly.

Anger laced across his face and he worked his jaw. "If I could have stopped what happened here, I would have. You must believe me."

Uncertain of what to say next, I nodded. Maybe he wanted some alone time. I definitely did. I was feeling really down, missing my parents something fierce.

"I think I'll go back to my room then," I said.

He eased himself away from the tree trunk. "After you, then."

A few paces inside the palace, I stopped, thinking I could benefit from some fresh air. Leaf too. I hadn't seen so many dead bodies before and needed to clear my mind. "What do you think about a quick walk?"

"It should be fine if we stay near the palace," he said.

Redirecting my path, I walked through the foyer, past the staircase, and outside to the garden in the back. Surrounded by the magical sights and smells of

Faevenly, I drew in a deep breath of the crisp, cool day. I held it for a few seconds before I let it trickle out of me. I did that a couple of times, trying to let my uneasiness fade, but it was hard. It stayed with me, like a heavy coat.

With a thick somberness surrounding us, I set off down the stone path. The pristine grounds of Strong Haven were tended by a crew of gnomes. Mom described them as small creatures about three feet tall with green skin and beady black eyes. They worked on the grounds in secret, and it was nearly impossible to spot one. They manicured the flowering shrubs and herbal plants and made sure the orbs floating around the paths stayed illuminated from dusk until dawn.

Glancing at the magical glowy balls, I asked, "Have you ever seen a garden gnome?"

"I have not."

We continued farther away from the palace. "I'd love to see one. If only for a second. My mom told me about seeing one once. Or twice. I can't remember."

Leaf kept following me in silence, and I wasn't sure if I should keep talking or let him enjoy the quiet. We passed a row of the sweetest smelling purple roses and I stopped to admire them.

"I feel the heavy loss too, Leaf," I said to him. "I understand."

"You cannot possibly understand how I feel," he whispered.

"If you talk to me, then maybe I can," I offered.

Sorrow flashed across his face, mirroring the

expression he had worn while the dead were being loaded onto the trailer. He backed away from me and seemed to steady himself. "I do not wish my pain on anyone, and I do not wish to share it. And if you know what is good for you, then you would do well to measure your interaction with me."

His emotion tugged at me, and an overwhelming desire to step closer to him ran through me, but I ignored it because I couldn't figure him out at all. And I needed to stop trying. "Fine," I finally said, turning away from him and continuing on.

We passed spraying fountains and concrete benches, croaking frogs, and singing birds. And when we had walked so far that the manicured grounds began looking wild and shadowy, he stopped me.

"This is beyond the property line. We need to go back," he warned.

I stopped and peered ahead. "You think there are more of those birds out there? What did you call them?"

"Raróg."

"Yes, Raróg. Do you think there are more of them out there?"

"Possibly, or something worse. Faevenly is filled with many creatures, and several of them are quite deadly."

A sprinkle of goosebumps raced down my arms as I imagined all the things nightmares are made of. All the things my mom and dad had apparently shielded me from. "Like soul vamps?"

"Among other things," he answered.

"What other things?" I asked.

He walked away slowly and let out an exasperated breath before turning back around to face me. "I almost forgot about your newfound interest in Faevenly."

"You know what, forget it," I said, spinning on my heels and heading back to the palace. A cool wind sifted through my hair as I thought of deadly fae creatures, trying to imagine what might be in the woods other than the Raróg. Probably nothing worse than the broody fae behind me.

And so I pretended like he wasn't protecting me. I went to my room and changed out of my silver dress and into the shirt and pants I had worn the day before. Feeling way more comfortable, I went to the small library on my wing of the palace, practically slamming the door in Leaf's face, and flopped on the couch. Surrounded by rich mahogany wood and rows and rows of shelves with the most interesting and beautiful hardbound books, I thought the space would make me feel better, but it didn't. Instead, I felt worse, because the room reminded me of the study back home.

I wondered how *Abuela* was doing. And where my parents were. And while I understood the importance of mourning, I was eager for the day to be over so Uncle Leto could let us know what he had in mind as far as the attack on Strong Haven and my parents.

Something needed to be done.

But then I realized something... I had a huge

resource of material around me. Books upon books filled with Faevenly history and lore. And so I got busy, thinking I could find something in these pages to help. Scanning the spines of the books, I started pulling them out and flipping through each one. I found a book with a string of strange-looking mathematical formulas, another with drawings of different types of horses, unicorns, and even a pegasus. Then I found a book on dragons. The pages had detailed drawings of different types of dragons and a write-up on the history of each one.

"Incredible," I murmured, not realizing Faevenly had dragons at one point. Aliana would've been in heaven in this library. I spent some time with the book, studying the drawings of dragons—massive ones with gold scales that were bigger than castles, long thin ones with green and yellow scales that lived in the water, medium ones of various coloring that looked normal size, whatever that was, and tiny purple and pink ones that were so small they looked like lizards with wings.

The book offered many different hypotheses for why dragons no longer roamed Faevenly. They migrated to another realm, they killed each other off, or they simply stopped reproducing, though there was no concrete proof for any theory. After a while, I put the book back, relieved that massive dragons didn't exist, but bummed that the tiny ones didn't.

I then started looking for something on soul vamps, wanting to learn more about Draven the witch and what it meant to be a creature like that. Eventually, I found a thick red leather-bound book that told the story of a soul vamp named Keres, the first witch ever to become a soul vamp. Engrossed in her tale, I read all about her and her sisters and how they were raised by harpies in a dark and wicked forest.

One day, when they were involved in a battle, Keres was wounded. She needed blood to survive and her sisters accidentally gave her the blood of a demonic shape shifter. And when she woke up, she was a soul vamp.

Unable to tear myself away from the tale, I ate my meals in the library while reading, immersed in Faevenly and the story of Keres.

As the day morphed into night and the orbs that provided light throughout the palace illuminated, I realized how exhausted I was. Finally leaving the library, with the book in hand so I could finish it later, I saw that Leaf had changed out of his silver clothes and was now wearing black pants with a white shirt, his long hair hanging loose behind his back. He shot me a curious look as he glanced at the book.

"Yes, I'm taking this book," I said. With his good looks infuriating me, I continued on to my room.

When I approached my room, scenes from the morning funeral suddenly replayed in my mind. Thoughts like that always seemed to magnify at night, and they were plaguing me now. Maybe it was anxiety that another strike could be imminent. Even though I could handle myself in case anyone else attacked Strong Haven, I'd need a weapon.

I finally gave Leaf my attention. "Do you have a sword or a stick I can have? Or a dagger?"

He tilted his head and studied me. "I do." He didn't move right away. His eyes held mine, searching, like he was deciding something.

I held out my hand. "Well, then."

He reached back for the fighting stick he wore slung behind his back and handed it to me. "Do you know how to use this?"

"Yeah, I got it." I took the weapon. "Thanks."

He offered me a slow nod, then stepped back.

Retreating into my room, I pressed my back against the door. I didn't understand Leaf at all. He was rude and arrogant, but also tender and caring. I wanted to know what thoughts swirled in his mind, what fears and worries he harbored. *Abuela* had said she couldn't read him. Now that I had spent some time with him, I understood what she meant.

Spotting a pitcher of rose-colored water and a tray of fruit, I set the stick down and went over and plopped a strawberry in my mouth. As I savored the flavors, my thoughts went to Leaf. If my *abuela* were here, she'd tell me to offer him some food. She considered sharing a meal and offering a meal acts of love and charity. Not that I loved Leaf or thought he needed charity. But offering him something to eat could be a peace offering and a chance for me to understand him. I didn't like being so mad at someone, and Mom always said to never go to sleep mad.

Picking up the tray, I went over to my door and opened it. Leaf was in his usual posture leaning against the wall, but straightened himself at my approach.

Stepping out into the corridor, I extended the tray. "I thought you might be hungry."

He considered my offering for a few seconds before taking a violet grape off the vine. "Thank you."

I waited a few seconds to see if he'd say anything else, but he didn't. "Good night, then."

I was turning to go back inside my room when he spoke. "Faevenly is filled with many different creatures."

Hiding a small smile, knowing my food offering had worked, I turned back around. "I'd love to hear about them."

He placed the grape in his mouth, then motioned at my tray. "May I hold that for you?"

"Sure."

He took the tray, then went back to leaning against the wall like I had found him, holding the tray so we could both graze from it. I stood across from him and leaned against the wall too.

"Before I explain about our creatures, what do you know of this realm?"

I sifted through all the stuff Mom and Dad had taught me when I was little but had a hard time recalling the details. "The fae realm overlaps the human realm, and we're separated by a thin veil in the middle called a stratus. And the stratus is where the shimmers come from."

"Very good," he said, taking another violet grape. "Anything else?"

"I actually just learned a lot about Faevenly in the library. I found a super interesting book on dragons and read about all the different ones that used to roam here." I took a small blueberry from the tray. It tasted a bit like peppermint mixed with chocolate. "Have you ever seen a dragon?"

"I have not. They lived long ago. Though I would love to have seen one. There are some who say they are hiding and will return one day. But no one knows for sure."

"That would be amazing if they returned," I mused.

"It could be, but it also could be terrible," he replied. "Did you learn anything else in the library? Anything about Torch Lake?"

"I didn't see anything on Torch Lake, but I know the area pretty well," I said, sifting through the grapes and taking an orange one. It burst with flavor in my mouth, reminding me of a tangerine.

"Then you know of the kelpies that inhabit the Mother of Rivers?"

He took a blueberry and I found myself mesmerized by his graceful hand movements, his long fingers, and the way his mouth moved when he chewed.

"The Mother of Rivers? Kelpies?" I asked, unfamiliar with those names, and turning my attention back to the tray.

"Mother of Rivers is what we call our waterways, as they are all connected. The kelpies keep an eye on things, and if there are any issues, they inform Lord Letormis."

"What's a kelpie?"

"Kelpies are water horses that can shift into other forms. They are creatures of solitude and prefer to be alone. Their magical powers are vast, and it is said they can summon floods if they are threatened."

"Wow, that's incredible. Have you ever seen one?"

"They are indeed incredible. And yes, I have seen one." He took a strawberry this time and took a small bite. "They can also be quite dangerous, much like every other creature in Faevenly."

The word dangerous took my thoughts to the other stuff I had learned in the library. "I found a book about a witch soul vamp named Keres."

His brows shot up. "What did the book say?"

"You know the story?"

"It is legendary and passed down through the tales. I have not read a book about Keres, though, and would very much like to see it sometime."

"Sure," I said, taking a blueberry. "I didn't get through the whole thing, because it's really long, but apparently Keres was the first witch to become a soul vamp. She was wounded in a battle and needed blood to survive. Her witch sisters took her to a magical forest where they killed a unicorn. They gave Keres the blood, but then later they found out the unicorn wasn't a unicorn, but a demonic shapeshifter. And then she woke up as a soul vamp."

"That pretty well sums up the story I have heard," he said.

The next few minutes passed in silence as we ate more fruit, and I found myself gazing at him in that dreamy way, getting lost in his beauty. Snapping out of it, I shifted my stance and asked, "Can you tell me more about Draven?"

His jaw clenched, and I could see anger rising in his eyes. "He is a deadly monster, and that is all there is to know about him." He pulled himself away from the wall and handed the tray to me. "The hour is late."

"Oh," I said, taking the tray, but I wasn't ready to end the conversation. I set the tray on the floor and moved in close. I didn't mean to strike a nerve. "Why do you get so angry sometimes?"

He looked away from me. "You would not understand."

"I think I would, if you let me try." His intensity drew me in, and I found myself moving closer to him. He matched my steps and came closer to me too.

"You do not want to consort with me, Gabriela," he warned. "I am no good."

"I think I can make up my own mind about what I want," I breathed.

The distance between us faded away until I was standing so very close to him. His spicy and woodsy smell was intoxicating, and I found myself getting lost in his dreamy blue eyes.

He brought his hand to my face and caressed me gently. "I am utterly fascinated by you, Gabriela. And try as I might to suppress my attraction for you, it seeps out of me."

"You're," I swallowed, "utterly fascinated by me?"

He licked his lips. "Yes."

His eyes studied mine before he closed the remaining distance between us. He kissed me, softly at first, and then with rising intensity as our lips met, our mouths opened, and our bodies pressed against each other. I didn't have much experience with this, but this... this felt so right. Standing there in his arms with my hands snaking up to wind themselves behind his neck was like finding something I didn't know I'd been missing.

I could've stayed like that much longer, but he gradually pulled away, hesitatingly, as if he was forcing himself to end our kiss.

"Good night, Gabriela," he said, pressing a final kiss to my forehead.

My lips tingled and my head soared, and I didn't know what to say. I picked up the tray from the floor. "Good night, Leaf."

Back in my room, I changed out of my clothes and slipped on my purple gown. The fabric hugged my skin like a soft pillow, and I felt like I floated into bed. With Leaf's staff next to me, I snuggled into the sheets. And when I closed my eyes, all I saw was him.

CHAPTER 12

A pitter patter of feet and a burst of sunlight on my face woke me in the morning. Cracking open my eyelids, I saw Gidna pulling back the curtains.

"It is a new day, my lady," she said with purpose. "And there is much to do."

"Already?" I asked with a yawn. "It feels like I've only been asleep for a few minutes." Lifting myself up a little, my arm slid against the stick Leaf had given me, reminding me that I had fallen asleep with it.

Gidna spotted the wood right away and her eyes went wide. "You slept with a weapon?"

"Yes," I answered, more defensively than I planned, sitting all the way up and rubbing my head. "I needed to be able to protect myself."

She moved over to the desk to get a fresh tray of food she must've set there. "I suppose I cannot argue with that. These are troubling times."

She brought the tray over and placed it on the table next to the bed. My eyes met a small serving of fruit along with a glass of green-hued water. "Last night you left me rose-flavored water. What flavor is this?"

"Celery," she answered, going over to the wardrobe

and pulling out several long dresses. "Could I interest you in a dress for today?"

"If it's okay, I prefer pants. They're more comfortable." With a wrinkle of my nose I whiffed the water, thinking it'd taste horrible, but found it light and refreshing.

She huffed. "Fine." She put the dresses back, then pulled out a stack of folded clothes. "Here is another pair of trousers and a tunic, then."

"Tunic," I said, pointing. "I keep calling it a shirt, but here it's a tunic."

She shook her head in an exasperated way, then set the outfit on the chaise. "Yes, it is a tunic. Now, please get dressed and ready quickly. Lord Letormis has called a meeting of his advisors for this morning in the study."

I perked up. "This morning, when?"

"As soon as you are ready. Everyone is arriving now."

"Now?" I jumped out of bed. "Gidna!" I was eager to get things going, but needed time to get ready for a formal meeting.

"You have time, my lady. Never fear."

After a quick trip to the washroom, I slipped on the dark purple pants that had a row of intricate emerald vines stitched on the sides and a black top with puffy sleeves and a low neckline with the same stitching on the cuffs and neckline. Someone had definitely elevated the work clothes style for me.

Rubbing the soft fabric, I said, "Thank you, Gidna. These are beautiful."

She nodded. "Befitting a princess, indeed. And looks lovely with your cross necklace and your gold hoop earrings. Now come over here so I can work on your hair."

She combed my long black and white-streaked locks, working them with droplets of a serum until my hair gleamed but wasn't the least bit oily. Then she braided a section on either side, pinning them together in the back. After that, she smoothed a light yet luxurious cream on my face, then swept color on my cheeks, eyelids, and lips. She stood back and admired her work.

"Lovely," she said. "Simply lovely."

I smiled at her. "Thank you, Gidna. I really do appreciate everything you're doing for me."

She blushed. "You are most welcome, my lady."

Taking my stick, I exited my room and saw Leaf across from my door. He was leaning against the wall, but stood erect when he saw me.

I cleared my throat. "Good morning, Leaf."

"Gabriela."

He moved close to me, and his fresh woodsy and spicy scent filled my senses in the most intoxicating way. He handed me a sling and in it was a stick like the one he had given me, but smaller.

"This fighting stick is better suited for your size and weight," he explained.

My eyes went wide. "Wow, Leaf, this is amazing," I said, stunned at his thoughtfulness. "Thank you."

"You are welcome." His eyes lingered on me for a moment before he stepped back.

For a moment, neither of us moved. The space between us felt different—charged in a way I couldn't quite explain. I became suddenly aware of how close he still was. Close enough that if I reached out, I could touch him.

I handed him his long stick and took the smaller one. It was about four feet long, made with rich red wood with a dark grain. It had a rounded tip on one end and a flat surface on the other. Balancing it on my open palms, the weight perfect —not too heavy, and not too light. He held up the dark leather sling so I could slip my arm through, then helped me position it on my back and sheath it in its place. He was efficient with his movements, but never rough.

He nodded. "We must go. Lord Letormis has called a meeting."

"I'm ready."

Leto's study was on the first floor of the palace. When we entered, we found Uncle Leto, Lady Sonia, a stocky dwarf with long red hair and a long beard, and a young fae with violet hair and blue eyes sitting around a large round table. They rose to their feet.

"Lady Gabriela," Uncle Leto motioned to the fae. "Allow me to introduce the head of security of Strong Haven, Dain." He then motioned to the dwarf. "And this is a master tracker I have called in for help, Githion."

"And this is Lady Gabriela," he said to them. "Daughter of Strong Haven and heir to the throne."

"My lady," they both said with a bow.

"Nice to meet you both," I replied, surprised at hearing myself referred to as heir to the throne, because I had never thought of myself like that. Though I supposed I technically was.

I moved closer to the table and took a seat. Leaf stood somewhere behind my chair. It was weird having him behind me during a meeting with others who could also protect me, so I turned around and motioned for him to take the chair next to me. He gave me a quizzical look, but sat down, keeping his back straight, and folded his hands on the table.

With everyone seated, Uncle Leto began. "Dain, tell us what you discovered after your investigation yesterday, beginning with our attackers. Were you able to gather information from any of the them?"

"No, my lord. There were no survivors. They all perished during the night. Some from their injuries, others by their own hand."

Githion raised a brow. "So, no one wanted to talk."

"Correct," Dain acknowledged.

"That is most unfortunate," my uncle said. "Tell us about your search then for Princess Celyse and Lord Julio."

"Of course," Dain said. "We have learned from witnesses that the princess and the lord were last seen in the corridors of the first floor, near the Great Hall. They were both armed with daggers, fighting off our attackers. It is unknown if they were injured, though our sources noted blood on their clothing and on their bodies. No one seems to know what happened to them from that point on."

My eyes watered over as I pictured my parents fighting for their lives and covered in blood. I swallowed, trying my best not to lose it, telling myself that they had been seen fighting, with weapons, and that was a good thing. It had to be a good thing.

"And you, Githion?" Uncle Leto asked. "What do you have to say?"

"My team and I have searched the grounds long and far, and we have found no trace of them." He brought his stare on me. "I assure you, my lady, we have not stopped searching. If they are out there, we will find them."

"Thank you, Githion," I said in a low tone, not saying anything about him using the word *if*.

"And what of Draven?" Uncle Leto asked. "What have you all found with regards to him?"

Dain answered first. "The dungeon has been triply inspected, and we found nothing out of the ordinary— no sign of witchery or spells, no unusual markings or tracks, no disturbance to the locks or bars of the room in which he was housed. It is as if Draven disappeared into thin air."

"Nonsense," Githion spat, banging his chunky fist on the wood table. "No one has ever disappeared from the Strong Haven dungeon. Not in all my years have I heard of such a thing!"

"I assure you, my findings are accurate," Dain sneered.

"It is true," Lady Sonia added in a calming voice. Her long dark hair, which she usually wore loose, had been pulled back into a braid. "No one has ever escaped our dungeon. And no one doubts your findings, Dain. I too have arrived at the same conclusion. But, Lord Letormis, we must keep in mind that the Strong Haven dungeon has never held the likes of Draven the witch. We had no reason to add new security measures over the years of his imprisonment."

"But why did he wait so long?" Uncle Leto asked, almost as if to himself. He sat back in his seat and crossed his arms. "He has been held for nearly twenty years. Twenty! Why escape now?"

Lady Sonia shook her head. "I wish I knew."

"Who can really understand the mind of a madman?" Githion asked.

A lull of silence set in as everyone considered why Draven had acted now, when Lady Sonia spoke. "I wonder something," she mused.

"What is that?" Leto asked.

Lady Sonia leaned forward. "What if Draven had help?"

"Help from within Strong Haven?" Dain asked with a furrowed brow.

"I cannot believe that!" Githion spat.

My stomach turned. Was there a traitor in the

palace? I didn't want to believe it either, but if a powerful witch had been locked up for so long, how else could he escape? I scanned the faces of everyone at the table, wondering if it was one of them, but having a hard time imagining it. No way was it Leto or Lady Sonia. Or even Leaf, he was with me when Draven escaped. My eyes rested on Dain and Githion. I supposed it could have been one of them, or another guard. Or maybe a maid servant.

Uncle Leto rose from his chair and paced about. "I too cannot believe such a thing, but I would be remiss in saying we should not look into it." He paused, his jaw tightening as if weighing the cost of his next words. "Githion and Dain, add it to your inquiries. But let no one know our suspicions. We do not want to create a panic. I expect answers as soon as possible."

"Aye," Githion answered.

"Of course, Lord Letormis," Dain said.

Uncle Leto folded his arms. "Now, to the matter of the meeting of the Council of Six, which is the reason why Lady Celyse and Lord Julio were here." He leaned forward, as if about to tell us a secret. We all moved in too. "I propose we go to the meeting as planned, representing the interests of Strong Haven, as planned. But instead of bringing Lady Celyse of Strong Haven"—he brought his attention to me—"we bring Lady Gabriela."

My stomach dropped as all eyes turned on me. "What?"

"The council is being convened for the purpose of

deciding if Strong Haven should remain the ruling province of Faevenly. I have our allies lined up to support our position—Lord Rook of the Sublands, House Lind of Cuesta, and possibly House Stromm of Summit Range. I strongly believe we can secure the Stromms with persuasion. But for this course of action to succeed, no one, not even our allies, can know what has happened here or that Princess Celyse and Lord Julio are missing. This knowledge could make us appear weak and vulnerable. Instead, we will present you, Lady Gabriela, as the head of the house and act as if there is nothing out of the ordinary."

All eyes were on me again, but this time they were filled with doubt more than anything else. I couldn't blame them. I wasn't my mother. I wasn't even sure I could be half of who she was. My stomach knotted, and the weight of their gazes pressed down like armor I wasn't strong enough to wear.

But beneath the fear, something else stirred—a flicker of defiance, small but steady. And the need to prove myself. They could doubt me all they wanted. I doubted myself, too. Yet somewhere deep inside, past the uncertainty and the ache, I didn't have the luxury of falling apart. Not now. Not when everything already breaking and my parents needed me.

"Lord Letormis, I mean no disrespect to Lady Gabriela, but will that work?" Dain asked. "Assuming we have the loyalties of three other provinces, which would secure a majority, will the other provinces recognize her authority?"

"House Kane of High Meadow will not," Githion asserted. "They have been eyeing the high seat for quite some time now."

"Then we crush them!" Leaf slapped his hands on the table. "The Kanes have long stood in our way and must be dealt with. And it would not surprise me in the least if they are the ones who somehow aided Draven in his escape." His voice rose with each word. "For all we know, Draven could be holding Celyse and Julio captive at their castle at this very moment."

Uncle Leto held out his hands and motioned for Leaf to calm down. "I know your grievances against the Kanes, and I share many of them, but there is a proper order to things. We cannot simply go in and attack them without proof of wrongdoing. But we *will* go to the meeting. We *will* glean as much information as possible. We *will* do whatever we can to make sure House Strong retains its position. And then, after that is secured, we *will* confront the Kanes."

"And what if we fail and House Strong loses the seat?" Leaf asked. "What if the Strongs are voted out and the Kanes take over?"

"Then"—Uncle Leto rubbed his face—"we abandon the council and pursue more aggressive tactics."

Leaf, Dain, and Githion looked as if they preferred the "abandon the council" approach, and honestly, I did too. If the Kanes had my parents, then we needed to go over there right away. But I trusted Uncle Leto. If my mom left him here to run things, then he should run things.

Right?

"What says Lady Gabriela?" Dain asked.

I blinked, my mind scrambling to catch up. Allies, provinces, councils—it was all so much bigger than me. They were talking about strategies and allegiances as if it were a chess game, and I didn't know what half the pieces were. My parents had been the ones who understood these things, who knew how to navigate the powers within Faevenly.

"Well," I began slowly, "it's hard for me to say anything, because I don't know the full history of the Kane family—only that they tried to take Strong Haven twenty years ago and were stopped by my parents."

"And they continue to meddle and plot and do whatever they can to undermine Strong Haven," Githion added with a grunt.

"I see," I said. "I want us to do whatever we can to keep our position in Faevenly, but my parents need me. If there's any chance to find them, then we need to take it."

"Your mother would want you to fulfill your duty to your house and attend the meeting," Uncle Leto said in a cautioning tone.

I swallowed. "Would she, Uncle?"

I didn't want to argue with him, but there was a reason why my parents ended up living in the human realm and rarely visited Faevenly. Was this it? Were they trying to protect themselves and me from the dangers of this realm, and especially the Kanes?

"If I may make a suggestion," Lady Sonia offered. "What if we do both? I propose we send a team to High Meadow to call on the Kanes, while at the same time we send Lady Gabriela and an entourage to represent our interests at the meeting."

Githion was quick to volunteer. "I will gladly go to High Meadow and pay a visit to the Kanes."

"And I as well," added Dain.

Uncle Leto met everyone's gaze before settling on mine. "Does that arrangement work for you, Lady Gabriela?"

I felt better with a group going to the Kanes' while Uncle Leto and the rest of us went to the meeting. That way, we covered our obvious bases. But I was also surprised that Uncle Leto had not made the suggestion himself. Was he hiding something?

"Yes," I said. "That works."

"Good. Then it is settled. Everyone prepare. We set out immediately."

Uncle Leto's command sent everyone moving, chairs scraping and voices rising in preparation. I stood, but my feet were rooted to the floor. Something in his tone didn't sit right. I glanced at Leaf. His expression was unreadable, but his hand brushed the hilt of his weapon as if he felt it too.

I followed the others out, my pulse heavy in my chest. We had a plan, but all I could think about was my parents—and the uneasy truth that not everyone in this room was telling me everything.

CHAPTER 13

Gidna had insisted I dress every part the princess for the meeting, and she was right. Pants wouldn't do. She whisked me away to the dressing room and primped me like it was prom night on steroids. With our impending departure, I was bathed, plucked, and lotioned at lightning speed. While my hair and face were being worked on, a trio of maid servants scurried in with the most stunning gowns I had ever seen. The colors were electric and the detail intricate; and they looked as if they had been made in the heavens.

"Wow," I gaped. "My mom mentioned the beauty of the gowns here, but I had no idea."

"They are a sight to behold, indeed. Now, make your selection quickly," Gidna prodded. "Time is wasting."

My choices included purple, blue, yellow, and green, with the green one standing out more than the others. It was a simple yet elegant silky sheath dress adorned with glittery gems, with thin straps and a plunging neckline. Leaf popped into my mind, and I wondered what he would think of me in it, but I quickly pushed that notion away. I needed to focus.

"The green one?" Gidna asked, pulling me away from my thoughts.

"Yes, the green one."

With my selection made and my primping finished, I stepped into the dress. It hugged my body perfectly, down to the petite length, and showcased my cleavage in a way I wasn't used to, but liked.

Gidna inspected me up and down, making sure everything was perfect. "Do you wish to wear your necklace?" she asked, nodding at my cross. "Or perhaps you would prefer one of sparkling jewels? I can provide matching earrings."

My faith was important to me, and having the cross on and visible made me feel better. As did my hoop earrings. "I prefer my own jewelry, but thank you. And by the way, how did you make a dress like this so quickly for me? It's the perfect size."

"We have our faerie ways," she said with a wink.

She darted about the room, placing a few things in a small bag, explaining everything she was packing, but my mind drifted away as uncertainty set in. I didn't know much about Faevenly, and here I was going into a huge meeting where all of Strong Haven depended on me.

"Gidna," I said in a half whisper. "What will happen if I fail and the Kanes take over?" Every moment we wasted was a risk. Like somewhere out there, something was getting closer.

She stopped in her tracks, as if she had run into a wall. "Do not speak thus. The sun, the moon, and the stars hear your words." She stepped closer to me, her eyes darting around nervously. "My dear, the Kanes are pure evil, power-hungry, and vile. They care not for nature, but only for wealth and power. All of Faevenly will suffer if they should be named the ruling house. Even the human realm will suffer, for they will do monstrous things with the shimmers. We cannot speak of such a despicable possibility. Understand?"

Shivers erupted down my arms, enhancing the low tingle that had never really left the back of my neck. I had never thought about someone using the shimmers like that. "They sound awful."

"They are, and that is why you will not fail, because you are good. Now come." She waved her hands in the air. "Enough of that talk. It is time for you to go."

I took my sling with my fighting stick and slipped it on while she handed me my bag and held the door open for me. When I stepped out into the corridor, Leaf was waiting. He had changed clothes too and wore black pants with a long-sleeved green tunic. With his long dark hair and piercing blue eyes, he looked incredible. He pulled back away from the wall slowly. His eyes stayed steady and cool, but I detected a distinct swallow at his throat.

"Lady Gabriela." His gaze lingered longer than it should have.

A warm flush crept up my cheeks while a flutter tickled my stomach. "Good morning, Leaf."

He followed me downstairs and outside to the carriages that were lined up along the circular gravel driveway. The same tall and magnificent horses from the funeral were leading the way.

"Um," I said, pointing at the magnificent beasts. "Don't those go to the Passing Place?" A nervous laugh escaped my lips. "I mean, we're not..."

"The Enbarr go wherever they are asked, if it pleases them," Leaf explained. "Today Lord Letormis has asked them to journey us to Strong Haven West for the council meeting."

Uncle Leto strolled up. "Leaf is correct. We are taking the Enbarr because we should have started on our way yesterday. But with everything that has happened, and with us setting out now, we needed the swiftest ride possible."

He pointed at a large black carriage. "I will travel with you and your attendant, Lady Sonia, in this carriage." He motioned at a smaller black carriage. "Leaf and a team of guards will be following."

I resisted glancing at Leaf as Uncle Leto placed his hand under my elbow and ushered me over to the carriage, feeling weird that my protector wouldn't be with me. I was getting used to him.

Leto held the door open for me. "Watch your step, my lady."

I climbed in and settled on the velvety smooth purple cushions, marveling at all the glistening wood. "It's really nice in here," I said to Lady Sonia, who climbed in next and sat next to me.

"Yes, the palace carriages are quite comfortable. Not that we will be in here long. Our journey will only take us a few hours, and we have many things to go over with you."

The carriage took off at a slow trot, then slowly gained speed, but our ride was never bumpy. Peering out the window, I saw flashes of landscape racing by, almost as if we were on a train.

"Incredible," I muttered.

Lady Sonia smiled. "It really is."

But I couldn't admire the ride for long, because soon Uncle Leto started preparing me for the meeting. "Back in the study, I mentioned our allies. Tell me their names and their provinces."

"You said Rook from the Sublands is an ally, but I don't know if that's his first name or last name."

"Rook is a first name and the only name he goes by, though his surname is Cailean. And yes, he is faithful to your mother and Strong Haven. He is also quite close with Leaf, as that is where Leaf lives."

"Leaf lives in the Sublands?" I almost did a double take. "I thought he lived in Strong Haven."

"He has never lived in Strong Haven. And though he calls the Sublands his home, he spends most of his time roaming Faevenly."

I wanted to ask more about Leaf, especially the roaming thing. Where did he roam, and why? What did he do and what was his connection to Rook? But I didn't dare veer from the lesson. Uncle Leto was in a mood, and I didn't think he'd like me asking about Leaf.

"Now, there is one other province with us," Uncle Leto said. "Who are they?"

"Well, you said, along with the Sublands, our ally is the Linds from Cuesta."

"Very good. And which province hangs in the balance?"

My mind churned as I struggled to remember the name. "Um, I think it was something like... Throm?"

"Stromm," Uncle Leto corrected. "The Stromm family is from Summit Range. Now, who is against us?"

"There are the Kanes from High Meadow, of course. And there are the fae from the Sands. The Bannons?"

He pinched the bridge of his nose. "The other province solidly against us is House Baffin from Sand Bluff. Now, please repeat the information."

Feeling like a complete idiot, I started rattling off the information when the constant tingle at the back of my neck amplified. My hands shot to the spot. Shivers raced up and down my body as a host of emotions swept over me.

"What is it?" Lady Sonia asked. She angled her body toward me, her eyes wide. "My lady, are you okay?"

Dark splotches covered my vision until I couldn't see. And then my body fell, as if in a free fall. I tumbled down into nothingness until I crashed onto solid ground. I stayed still, trying to get my bearings.

"Mija."

I blinked, looking for the voice, because I knew it right away. "Dad?" I whispered into what seemed like a void. "Is that you?"

A soft light broke up the darkness. It grew ever so slowly until my dad came into view. I pushed off the ground and rushed into his arms, hoping this wasn't a dream.

"Dad!" My voice choked over. "You're okay!"

He hugged me tightly and I smelled his familiar fresh, soapy scent. "I am, *mija*. I am." He drew back and cupped my face in his hands, smiling at me with the saddest eyes.

My gut sank. "What is it?" Looking around, I saw the darkness had disappeared, and in its place glowed a lavender-filled meadow, stretching as far as the eye could see. But Mom was nowhere in sight. "Where's Mom?"

His eyes watered. "Listen to me carefully, because I don't know how long my mind can keep you here."

Looking down at myself, I saw my now fuzzy body glimmering, like a dream, while his seemed firm. "I'm not really here," I murmured. "But how can I touch you?"

"Our connection is strong, and I have to assume it's one of our Avila gifts. And no, you are not here. But your mother and I are. Our bodies are physically in this place." He looked around. "I'm not sure what it is, but I think it's a sort of limbo, or a realm I've never heard of."

An icy blast of fear shot through me. "Limbo, as in, where dead people go? Dad…" Tears flooded my throat and rushed my eyes. "Are you and mom… dead?"

He shook his head. "I don't know exactly *what* we are. I haven't been able to figure it out, but that's not what's important right now. Listen carefully, because I don't know how long I can keep our connection." He moved in close. "When the palace was attacked, your mother and I came face to face with Draven the witch. Before we ended up here, he taunted us with the knowledge that someone helped him escape. One of our own."

A gasp escaped my lips and my body trembled. "We thought a traitor might have helped him. But it was just a theory I didn't want to believe."

Dad nodded. "I didn't want to believe it either, I still don't, but I believe it's true."

"Do you have any idea who it is?"

"None. As far as your mother and I know, everyone at Strong Haven is trustworthy… or was trustworthy." He shook his head. "It makes no sense."

My mind reeled as I grappled with the implication of what my dad was telling me. "What do I do?"

He moved in close. "Do not tell anyone you came here, or that you talked to me, or that you have confirmation there is a traitor in Strong Haven." He paused, his words sinking in. "Do not trust anyone. Okay?"

"Okay," I looked around again, hoping to catch a glimpse of Mom. "But Dad, where's Mom?"

He swallowed. "Please don't worry about her or me. I've got this. But you, you need to..."

My mind zipped back to my body with a jerk as I was flung forward and face-planted into Uncle Leto's chest. He wrapped his arms around me, cradling me to cushion my fall. Shrieking from the Enbarr outside exploded in my ears as our carriage jumped and skidded out of control. Lady Sonia's body rammed against the wood next to me, her eyes wide with alarm. The carriage spun and weaved, creaking and moaning, before screaming to halt.

The Enbarr whinnied and brayed, the sound of their crashing hooves loud, but then becoming softer as they drifted away. Silence descended, but not for long. Shouting rang out followed by the whizzing of arrows and the clashing of weapons.

"We're under attack," I whispered.

Uncle Leto pulled an onyx dagger from his belt and freed the stick he had slung at his back. "Stay here," he warned Lady Sonia and me, before opening the carriage door and jumping out.

I kept still, frozen by disbelief, but only for a few seconds. I could fight and they needed me. I reached for my stick, unsheathing it quickly.

"My lady Gabriela, it is not safe," Lady Sonia warned.

"I know. But I'm going."

Jumping out after Uncle Leto, I saw a group of men in black hooded cloaks closing in. Leto charged them, swinging his stick in one hand and his dagger in the other. Leaf and his men were behind us, charging at another group of attackers. Like a graceful warrior, Leaf wielded his weapon with ease, spinning and lunging with agility and precision, as if performing a deadly yet beautiful dance. He parried and charged, then must have sensed me, because his gaze caught mine. His eyes widened with fear.

"Gabriela, behind you!" he yelled.

I ducked and spun out of the way as an arrow whizzed over my head. I righted myself quickly and saw a large fae bearing down on me with a long black stick. I deflected the blow with my own weapon, then kicked him between his legs. He toppled over, but not before another one appeared. Breaking to the right, I drew him away, then doubled back quickly and crouched so that he tumbled over me. I raised my stick and brought it down on his throat.

"Kill the princess!" yelled another attacker, racing toward me. I held my ground, staring him down, ready to strike, when a barrage of arrows whisked by me and thudded into his head and chest. He stood there for a few seconds, then collapsed to his knees and fell over. Leaf ran to my side, his bow and arrow ready for more unleashing.

"What are you doing out here?" he hissed, pressing his back toward mine as we moved in perfect harmony.

Catching my breath, I managed to get out, "I'm fighting!"

Another cloaked figure approached from the side, but was too close for Leaf to fire off an arrow. Instead, he gripped the attacker's stick and swung at his head. With the fae stumbling, Leaf and I spun, allowing me a perfect throw with the dagger. With a hard fling, I struck him in the chest.

We stayed like that, back to back, until the other Strong Haven guards approached. Leaf joined them, and together they formed a circle around me, shielding me from any other dangers that might still be out there.

"Is that all of them?" Leto asked, scanning our surroundings.

Leaf ticked his chin at the guard beside him. "Take one other guard and check the perimeter."

The guard and the one next to him took off. Uncle Leto turned to face me and furrowed his brow. "I told you to stay put, Gabriela."

"I know what you told me. But you needed more fighters, so I helped."

He rubbed his forehead then fixed me with a hard stare. "Your protection is paramount- above anything else. And you will do as I tell you. Understood?"

I paused for a second, not at all appreciating his tone, but knew better than to challenge him at this moment. "Understood."

Lady Sonia emerged from the carriage. She lifted the train of her long red dress, moving about the bodies. "If there are survivors, we can question them," she said.

Uncle Leto joined her, poking and prodding our

attackers with his stick, but none of them moved. "All dead," he announced.

The two that had left to check the perimeter returned. "There are no others," one of them said.

Uncle Leto looked ready to explode. "First, they came for Lady Celyse. Now, for Lady Gabriela. In the human realm with the soul vamp, in the forest with the Raróg, and now this carriage attack. It is quite clear that Strong Haven is not wanted at the meeting of the Council of Six. The question is, who is responsible? The Kanes or the Baffins?"

"Or Draven," Lady Sonia suggested.

"Or all three," Leaf said.

Or Draven and one of our own, I thought, my dad's confirmation about a traitor blaring in my head.

CHAPTER 14

Our attackers were dead, but so were some of our guards. And all of our Enbarr had run, though one had ventured back. Uncle Leto wasted no time issuing orders, because we needed to get to Strong Haven West as soon as possible.

"We will prepare the dead for the Passing Place ourselves," he said. "Then we will make haste."

The bodies of our attackers and our own men were carried away from the road and into a grassy area surrounded by a flowering field and berry bushes. They were lined up, side by side, their hands folded over their chests and their eyes closed. Any visible signs of blood or grime were wiped away and their clothes and hair straightened.

When we finished, we stood silent for a few long minutes.

Leaf stayed farther back than everyone, like he had at the ceremony at Strong Haven. Deep pain etched across his beautiful face, like before. He met my gaze for a brief second but quickly dropped it and looked away. But I didn't keep my thoughts on him. I couldn't. I had too much on my mind, with my dad's sad eyes and worried expression playing over and over in my brain. He had wanted to say more, but our connection was severed when we were attacked. I wished I knew where they were and what he was going to say.

"Back to the carriage," Uncle Leto announced, leading everyone away from the meadow. When we got there, he addressed us all. "We fill up the large carriage as best we can and use the remaining Enbarr to transport us. Everyone else will journey on foot back to the east."

While a couple of guards piled into the carriage, Uncle Leto and Lady Sonia soothed the Enbarr and secured it back to the carriage. As I watched them, Leaf came over to me.

"Are you well?" he asked.

"I am, and thank you. You saved me, Leaf, for the second time."

With the pain from the losses still on his face, he said, "Do not thank me."

Leaf stepped back as Uncle Leto opened the carriage door. I climbed in and slid onto the seat beside one of the guards, with Lady Sonia settling next to me. Leaf took the seat across, and Uncle Leto and another guard entered last. Once the door closed, he gave a sharp whistle. The Enbarr started at a steady trot, then shifted smoothly into its magical sprint, the world outside blurring into streaks of color.

Uncle Leto started laying out the plan. "Weapons and guards are not allowed in the manor house, so everyone will be outside while Lady Gabriela, Lady

Sonia, Leaf, and myself go in unarmed. I want both guards as close to the structure as possible. Stay together. Do not separate, and do not, under any circumstances, congregate close to any of the guards of the other houses. Stay sharp and alert. If a scuffle should break out during the meeting, then protocol will have been abolished. You will charge in, weapons at the ready. Gabriela and her survival are our top priority. No other life is as important. Not mine, nor anyone else's. Understood?"

"Yes, my lord," the guards said together.

With my uncle finished with his instruction, everyone fell quiet. Only the whirring from the racing carriage wheels over the dirt and grass could be heard, along with the occasional creaking of the wood.

I started whittling at my freshly manicured nails, feeling way too unimportant to be thought of as a top priority, and wished my parents were here instead. Mother was a princess; she knew how to act like one and what to say. She could handle anything. I was just a girl in high school, planning for college. But I guess I really wasn't anymore. Now I was a fae princess with my life on the line, being hunted. And my parents were in some sort of limbo.

As my mind swirled, I detected a slowdown in the carriage's speed. My nerves escalated and my heart raced. What if I messed everything up? What if more died because of me? Lady Sonia must've sensed my fear, because she reached out, slipped her hand around mine, and squeezed. Her touch made me feel better, and I squeezed back when a terrifying thought occurred to me.

I didn't want her to be the traitor, but what if she was?

The carriage rolled to a soft stop. Uncle Leto opened the door and hopped out. Lady Sonia and I were next, followed by Leaf and the other guards.

The sun was shining bright when we left Strong Haven East, but here in the West, it had disappeared. Thick gray clouds filled the daytime sky, and a misty fog hovered close. My gaze followed a long line of carriages that wrapped around a gravel circular drive, then swept up to a massive white three-story stone mansion. Flowering pink vines framed the impressive double wood door, and flowering bushes of all shapes and sizes clustered around the facade.

"We are late," Uncle Leto murmured. "Come on, then."

"Leto!" someone called out. "Do not go in there!"

Uncle Leto kept walking, as if he hadn't heard the warning. But I had. I grabbed his arm and pulled him to a stop. "Someone just yelled for you to not go in."

His eyes darted around. "Who?"

"I don't know." I surveyed the guards standing around, wondering who had called out, but no one made any indication. Then I saw them. Two opaque but fuzzy forms came into view, becoming more visible with each step. They dashed our way from a cluster of trees. Two dead fae warriors, a guy and a lady, with long dark braided hair.

"You can hear us!" the fae lady said excitedly with wide eyes.

"I can. I can see y'all too."

"She said y'all," the guy said to the lady. "She must be from the human realm, and from Texas."

"Are you?" the lady asked. "From the human realm?"

"I am, from Austin, Texas to be exact."

Uncle Leto came up to me. "Gabriela? Is someone here?" he asked, looking about.

"Tell him it is Ferna and Parlan," the fae guy instructed.

"They say they are Ferna and Parla," I said. Then I added, "they are standing in front of you."

A look of happiness mixed with sadness covered my uncle's face. "My dear friends." He searched the empty space. "I am so glad to know you are here." He glanced at the mansion. "I can only assume something is afoot? What news do you have?"

"Something indeed," Parlan said. "We noticed the arrival of the carriages and saw a representative of each house enter. We thought your delay was suspicious so went in and listened in on many conversations. We learned that today you will vote on the high council seat, and every province's representative, with the exception of Rook, is with the Kanes."

My stomach dropped as I relayed the message slowly, careful not to miss any part of what the fae had said.

"Everyone except Rook? Even the Linds?" Uncle Leto asked with surprise. "Are you certain?"

"We are certain," Ferna answered.

I repeated her confirmation as Uncle Leto exchanged a glance with Lady Sonia. "Thunderation," he muttered. "We have been betrayed."

Leaf worked his jaw, and a guttural growl escaped his lips. He looked like he wanted to explode. "The Kanes will never stop their treachery."

Uncle Leto placed his hand on Leaf's shoulder. "All is not lost. We have Lady Gabriela. With her at our side, the vote may go against the Kanes."

"They should have been dealt with long ago," Leaf warned.

"Perhaps, but there is nothing we can do about that now," Uncle Leto said. "We need to see this course of action through."

"I agree," Lady Sonia tacked on. "We need to stick to the plan and pray to the sun, the moon, and the stars that our alliances will hold firm with us when they see us."

Their words echoed in the still air, heavy with a mix of hope and fear. I wanted to believe in alliances and plans and prayers—but deep down, it felt like we were holding everything together with the thinnest threads. Every decision carried the weight of lives, and I was tangled in the middle of it all, expected to lead a realm I barely understood.

"Let's see what happens," I muttered.

Uncle Leto, Lady Sonia, Leaf, and I walked to the

house, as did Ferna and Parlan. As the cool wind swirled in the misty air, the mood from Leaf also swirled. I could feel the anger coming off him like a thick cloud. And I couldn't blame him. Other than Draven, it seemed like the Kanes were responsible for a lot of turmoil in Faevenly, both when my parents were last here and continuing now.

I brought my hand to the cross that hung around my neck and said a silent prayer for the meeting to go our way. Because something told me it wouldn't.

CHAPTER 15

A tall, thin woman with silver hair pulled up in a bun and wearing a long black dress greeted us at the door. She wore a smile of formality and authority and gave us a simple nod as she motioned us inside.

"Lord Letormis, Lady Sonia, it is lovely to see you both." Her glance grazed mine as she looked beyond me through the open door. "Where are Lady Celyse and Lord Julio?"

"They were unable to make it," my uncle answered. "They have sent their daughter, Lady Gabriela, in their stead."

Her eyebrows shot up. "My, my. What a lovely surprise." She closed the door and turned to face me. "Lady Gabriela, it is my pleasure to meet you at last. I am Lady Wren." She bowed her head low. "I take care of Strong Haven West for House Strong and have been its custodian for quite some time now."

"It's very nice to meet you, Lady Wren," I smiled, trying not to show my rocketing anxiety over the meeting. "Thank you for everything you do and have done for my family," I said, trying to act the part of a Strong Haven princess.

"I see from the line of carriages that everyone is here," my uncle cut in, getting straight to business.

"Indeed they are," Lady Wren answered. "And have been for quite some time. I should warn you that their patience has been running thin. I fear a tumultuous meeting may be afoot."

Uncle Leto grumbled, then muttered in a low voice. "I am sure."

"Come," said Lady Wren. "I will show you in, but as per established protocol, is everyone unarmed? I must hear from each individual."

"I am unarmed," Uncle Leto announced. He nodded at me to say the same thing and I did, followed by Lady Sonia and then Leaf. Since fae couldn't lie, I figured the verbal statement assured no weapon made its way inside. But since I was only part fae, I could lie all I wanted. Not that it mattered. We had all left our weapons in the carriage.

"Very good," said Lady Wren. "Allow me to show you to the receiving room."

She ushered us across the all-marble foyer and into a big room with shiny dark wood floors and a strong scent of pine in the air. Soft green walls sparkled with an iridescent sheen, and rich gold drapes framed the windows that lined the back walls. A large round table took up most of the room, and it was surrounded by several lords and one lady, all dressed in their finest. They rose to their feet when we walked in.

"Apologies for our delay," Uncle Leto said, waltzing into the room with confidence. "You all know Lady Sonia and Leaf. And this"—he motioned to me—"is Lady Gabriela of House Strong, daughter of Lady Celyse and Lord Julio. She is representing Strong Haven today."

A tall, thin guy with long jet-black hair and piercing blue eyes rose to his feet. "And where is Lady Celyse? We were expecting her."

"Lady Gabriela," my uncle Leto said to me as he motioned to the man. "This is Lord Alexander Kane of High Meadow. And Lord Kane, Lady Celyse could not be here but sends this daughter of Strong Haven with full authority."

A muscular man with long, full dark hair and thick brows stood. He looked more like a linebacker and less like a fae. "I am Rook of the Sublands, Lady Gabriela. I am honored to meet you and accept your authority here."

"Thank you," I said, grateful to have at least one supporter.

From the corner of my eye, I noticed Leaf moving along the perimeter of the room with soft steps, coming to a halt behind Lord Kane. Ferna and Parlan were close to him. Was he worried the Kanes would do something?

I stilled my breathing and tried to connect my mind to Alexander's like *Abuela* had taught me in the kitchen. I wanted to see what he was up to, but my thoughts were all over the place. Though I didn't exactly have to connect to him to know what he thought of me. His frown and his upturned nose said it all.

"I accept Lady Gabriela," a beautiful and delicate younger fae with long silver hair said. "I am Lady Fayette Lind of Cuesta."

"Thank you," I nodded, relieved to see another lady with authority. Maybe she would stand with me.

"I am Lord Barent Stromm of Summit Range, and I too have no issue with Lady Gabriela." He had long dark hair worn in a singular braid. Even though he spoke to me, he avoided direct eye contact.

Definitely not a good sign.

"Same for me," another fae chimed in with silver hair worn in a trio of thick braids. "I am Lord Evan Baffin of Sand Bluff, Lady Gabriela."

Uncle Leto cupped his hand under my elbow and ushered me to two empty seats. I sat slowly, and he joined me, while Lady Sonia stayed behind my chair. Everyone around us sat too, with Alexander being the last to lower himself.

Uncle Leto cleared his throat. "I would like to begin the meeting with—"

"We have been here long and are ready to vote," Lord Kane interrupted with an imposing glare. "We do not need any opening statement."

Rook pounded his fist on the table. "I am not ready to vote. I would like to hear what Lord Letormis has to say."

"I would not," Alexander snapped. "And I believe

everyone here, with the exception of yourself, feels the same way."

A surge of panic swirled inside of me. Ferna and Parlan were right. The arrogant Kane had everyone in his pocket, except for Rook. If we voted now, he would win. My mind was scrambling for what to say and what to do when Leaf pounced. He grabbed Alexander from behind, slammed one hand on the top of his head and the other on his chin, then jerked. Alexander slumped over—dead.

Gasps broke out. Shouts erupted. Uncle Leto sprang to his feet. He grabbed my hand and yanked me out of my chair, pulling me to the door. Before we darted out, several fae jumped Leaf.

"Leaf!" Uncle Leto yelled. "Get out of there!"

With Lady Sonia on our heels, we dashed through the foyer and burst outside. "Prepare the carriage!" Uncle Leto yelled.

We sprinted past the confused guards of the other provinces and were almost to our ride when the fighting from the mansion spilled outside.

"Stop them!" someone yelled from the front door.

"Thunderation," Uncle Leto spat. He flung open our carriage door, practically pushing me and Lady Sonia inside. He grabbed his stick from the seat, then funnelled our guards in. With the carriage almost full, Uncle Leto hopped in but kept the door open.

"Come on, Leaf," he urged under his breath while peering out the door. "Come on."

An arrow whizzed through our window, lodging

over my head with a thunk. I ducked while one of our guards unleashed a barrage of arrows in return.

"We should go!" Lady Sonia called out. "Now!"

"No! We need to wait for Leaf!" I rushed out.

Not one second later, Leto called, "I see him!"

Leto let out two short whistles, and the Enbarr started backing up. When the carriage had reversed enough, it swung around with a jostle as Leaf jumped in. Cuts laced his face and blood splashed his shirt. Leto slammed the door closed and yelled, "Ride!"

The Enbarr bolted, sending everyone flailing until the rhythm transitioned to a steady speed. I clutched my cross, breathing heavily, then gaped at Leaf sitting on the other side of Lady Sonia, bruised and bloodied.

"Oh, my gosh. Leaf, are you okay?" I asked.

Before he answered, Uncle Leto bellowed, "What were you thinking!?"

Leaf didn't flinch. He didn't even move. He leveled a look at my uncle. "Alexander had converted everyone there, except for Rook. If they had voted, it would have gone against Strong Haven. I stopped the vote and finally did what should have been done long ago."

Uncle Leto sat back. He pressed the palm of his hand to his forehead. "I cannot talk to you right now. You will hold your tongue until we get back to the East."

Leaf folded his hands on his lap and stared down at the floorboard of the carriage. He didn't say a word. Neither did anyone else. We were shocked.

Lord Alexander Kane was dead, and I had no idea what that meant. Other than it wasn't good. Not at all.

CHAPTER 16

The ride to Strong Haven felt like an eternity. Tension hung thick in the air and my nerves stayed on high alert. Even the tingling at the back of my neck had heightened in intensity. I turned my thoughts to my dad, and my *abuela*. I needed them now more than ever, because I had no idea what was going to happen to us now.

The carriage finally slowed down, rolling to a stop in front of Strong Haven Palace. Uncle Leto opened the door with a jerk and hopped out. He walked in a small circle as the carriage emptied.

"To your stations," he ordered the guards.

They left, leaving me, Lady Sonia, and Leaf with my uncle. When the guards were out of earshot, Leto got up in Leaf's face. "Do you know what you have done? Do you have any idea?"

"Leto, please," Lady Sonia pleaded, tugging on the back of his shirt.

He silenced Lady Sonia with a wave, keeping his glare on Leaf. But Leaf didn't answer. Finally, Leto backed off. "Get cleaned up. Then meet me in the study."

"Yes, my lord," Leaf uttered.

Leaf turned and walked around to the back of the palace. I wanted to go after him but didn't want my uncle to know. I didn't think he'd approve after what Leaf had done.

"I, uh, need a moment in my room." I glanced down at my gown. "And I need to change clothes."

Uncle Leto nodded. "Be quick about it. We have much to discuss. But before you go, I need to ask you a question."

I froze, feeling as if I was in trouble. Like I had been caught sneaking out of the house or something. "What is it?"

"Back in the carriage, on the way to the West before we were attacked, you had one of your father's episodes. I could see it in your eyes. What was it?"

I could lie all I wanted, and Uncle Leto knew, so I had to turn on my acting skills and say something believable. My hand crept to the back of my neck. "Oh yeah, I had a really strong vibe. It caught me off guard and freaked me out a little, and then our carriage was attacked."

"I see," Uncle Leto said. "So you think it was a warning about the attack?"

"Yeah, it had to be."

"I suppose," he muttered.

Then, to solidify my story, I deflected. "Why? Do you think it meant something else?"

He rubbed his chin while keeping his attention on me. "I do not know."

"Me neither," I said. Then I took a couple of steps away. "If it's okay with you, I'm going to my room now. I need to wrap my head around everything that just happened. Send for me when you need me."

He softened his eyes and placed his hands on my shoulders. "You were brave today, Princess Gabriela. I am very proud of you."

"Thank you, Uncle," I said, rubbing his hands.

I walked through the front doors of the palace, crossed the foyer, passed the stairs, and went out the back to the garden. Picking up my pace, I rounded the path to the cook house, thinking Leaf had gone there since it was near the healing chamber, when I nearly collided with him.

"Leaf."

He took two steps away from me. "Gabriela."

A flutter of nervousness coursed through me, and I found myself wanting to get closer to him. "I, uh, wanted to catch up to you to see if you were okay."

He sidestepped around me and continued walking. "I am fine."

I reached for his sleeve and tugged. "Wait a minute. No you're not, and we should probably talk about it."

He stopped, but stayed in his place, refusing to turn around and face me. "There is nothing to talk about."

I moved around in front of him. Suddenly, everything I'd been feeling spilled out of me.

"There's a lot to talk about, Leaf. You are impulsive, rude, impossible to understand, and sometimes you irritate the hell out of me!" My chest heaved with emotion as strong affection for him took over my better judgment. I drew in a deep breath and steadied myself, then reached out for his fingers. "But you are also filled with passion and feeling, and I know what you did back there was at least partially for me. I understand, Leaf."

Hurt flashed across his face and filled his wounded eyes. "You do not know me and cannot possibly understand why I do the things I do."

I swallowed. "I'd like to try, if you'd let me."

"It is too late for that. Too late for me. What I have done cannot be undone." He swallowed, then cast his gaze away from me. "I hope you will forgive me, Gabriela. And I pray you stay away from me. I am no good for you."

This time, I let him walk away while a multitude of emotions cascaded over me—anger, affection, confusion. And I wondered if our kiss meant anything to him.

I continued down the path, walking farther into the garden, and came upon a stone bench. Sitting alone, I stared into the distance as images from the meeting invaded my mind like a scene from a horror movie stuck on replay. A movie I didn't want to watch anymore, let alone star in. But unfortunately, I was stuck.

"My lady!" Maid Gidna called, pattering over to me from the other end of the garden. "I have heard the news!"

I walked over to her. "Oh, Gidna. It was awful."

"I can only imagine." She hugged me tight and I held on to her for a bit, taking comfort in her embrace. She slowly pulled away. "Word is spreading that we will be attacked. Lord Letormis has ordered everyone to prepare. He has called a meeting with his advisors."

"Yes, I know. I told him to send for me when they were ready."

"That is why I am out here. He told me to fetch you. Now come with me so you can prepare."

Her stocky legs moved quickly, leading me into the palace, up the stairs, and to my room. Instead of the usual trio of maid servants that always seemed to assist Maid Gidna, there was only one in my room. A small maiden with short brown hair filled with flowers and leaves. She held a large silver tray with a washrag, a large towel, and small bottles of oil.

"Off with that dress," Maid Gidna ordered. "You will sponge your body then apply fresh oil and a new outfit."

I pulled the delicate fabric over my head and tossed it on my bed, keeping on my undergarments. The maid servant handed me the washrag. The warmth soothed my skin and a burst of lavender and gardenia filled my senses while I wiped my face and neck, then moved the cloth across my arms, body and legs. When the rag turned cool and the lavender scent faded, I handed it back to her. She took it and extended the towel.

Drying off, I studied the young maiden's face. "What is your name?" I asked, realizing it was rude of me not to ask, and also realizing I hadn't asked the other maid servants for their names.

She bowed her head. "I am Balina, my lady." She extended the tray, showing me the oils. "Would you like to pick your fragrance now?"

With a nod, I studied the tray. It held three vials—a shiny pink one, a sparkly white one, and a dark purple one. My mood hung dark, like the purple glass. I took it and opened it, then brought it up to my nose. My senses connected with a rich, sweet, floral aroma with strong notes of woodsy spice. I dabbed the oil on my wrists, behind my ears, and on the part of my hair like my mom had shown me when I was little.

"Thank you, Balina."

Maid Gidna shooed Balina away, then opened the wardrobe. "What would you like to wear? A dress? Or pants?"

"Another dress," I said, wanting to assume full princess mode. "But nothing too fancy."

"Excellent," she said, sifting through the choices and bringing out a dress. It was a simple, sleeveless long red dress with scoop neckline.

"That's perfect, Gidna. Thank you."

With the dress on, I slipped my feet into matching red slippers and drew in a deep breath. I dreaded going to the meeting. Was beyond scared of what Alexander's death meant not only for me, but for Strong Haven too. On top of that, I was sick with worry about my parents, especially since I had no idea where they were and if they were really okay.

Then there was Leaf.

"Are you ready to go downstairs?" Maid Gidna asked, interrupting my grim thoughts.

"I guess," I muttered.

"I guess nothing!" she harrumphed, raising her soft voice. "You are a daughter of Strong Haven, and right now the leader of this house." She stomped her heavy foot for emphasis. "You are ready for anything and everything."

Of course, she was right. I was the daughter of a fae princess and a human witch. Even though I didn't understand the gifts I possessed, they still belonged to me. And if my *abuela* was right, like she always was, my gifts would be there for me when I needed them. They had to be.

"Thank you, Gidna. Thank you for reminding me that I'm a badass."

Her mouth dropped open and Balina chuckled. "Now, now, my lady," Maid Gidna said. "I never said anything about your backside."

I smiled. "It's an expression that means I'm tough. It's not really about my backside."

"Oh," she said. She leaned in and lowered her voice. "Well, you are a badass. Just like your mother. And father too."

Feeling better about things, I took the stick and the sling Leaf had given me and positioned them on my back. I was ready for that meeting, and ready to fight for my parents and my Faevenly home.

CHAPTER 17

When I stepped out of my room, I was met by a guard I didn't recognize. It was strange seeing him there instead of Leaf, but I forced the broody fae out of my mind. If he wanted me to forget him, then I'd forget him.

I had plenty of other things to worry about.

Walking with determination and approaching Leto's study, I slowed when I neared the door. Four guards stood on alert, backs against the wall and eyes sharp. As I walked through the door, I found guards inside too. Along with my uncle, Lady Sonia, and Leaf.

"Ah, Lady Gabriela," my uncle said. "Please sit. We have a great deal to discuss."

I took my place at the table and folded my hands on my lap. Scanning the room, I saw Lady Sonia had changed from her red dress to a blue one. Uncle Leto wore the same dark brown pants and shirt with a dark cloak, and Leaf had changed into black pants with a green shirt. I had no idea how, but even with his cuts and bruises he still looked gorgeous with his perfect high cheekbones and full lips.

Not that it mattered.

Uncle Leto wasted no time starting the meeting. "I have received three owl-couriered messages. One came from Githion and Dain, informing me that they were allowed a visit at the House Kane palace with no incident and, unfortunately, with no sign of Lady Celyse nor Lord Julio."

Of course, I knew my parents weren't there, but found it interesting that Githion and Dain were allowed in so easily. "I assume they got there and left before everything happened at Strong Haven West?"

"It appears so," Lady Sonia replied. "Which is a blessing. They would have been executed on sight otherwise."

"They would have indeed," muttered Uncle Leto, casting a side eye to Leaf who remained quiet in his chair.

"What were the other messages?" I asked.

"Rook from the Sublands is on his way here with his full battalion of warriors," Leto said. "He is loyal to House Strong and will stand with us."

I swallowed. "Stand with us?"

"Yes," Leto explained. "Stand with us, as the third message came from House Kane, Alexander's father to be exact. They have issued a declaration of war against Strong Haven, with the full support of the remaining houses."

I wasn't surprised, but still my stomach sank and my nerves rocketed. This was bad.

Leto rose to his feet and paced the room. "If House

Kane comes with House Lind, House Baffin, and House Stromm, then..."

"Then we must be ready," Leaf said with conviction, finishing Leto's sentence.

"Even if we are ready, and with the Sublanders on our side, it will still be four houses against two. Those are losing odds no matter how you look at it," Leto said.

"Not if we're stronger than them," Leaf said. "A smaller force can defeat a larger force *if* they are stronger."

I tilted my head and studied him. "What do you mean, *if* they are stronger?"

Leaf shifted in his seat. He answered me, but kept his attention on Leto. "If we can find some aquoise, the other houses will not stand a chance against us."

Lady Sonia scoffed. "Come now, Leaf. You know very well that all of the aquoise in Faevenly has been depleted."

"Um, can someone please tell me what aquoise is?" I asked, feeling completely lost.

"It is a stone," Uncle Leto said to me. "A blue stone that when ingested gives immense physical strength for a finite amount of time. It used to be in abundance in Faevenly, but no longer." He swung his attention back on Leaf. "And I do not know why you would make such a suggestion, knowing it does not exist anymore."

"It may not exist here," Leaf explained. "But I believe there may be some in the human realm."

Lady Sonia leaned forward, her brows raised. "The human realm? Why do you think so?"

"Twenty years ago, when everything happened with Celyse and Julio, I spent some time with them in the Sublands caves. While there, we gathered a number of aquoise stones. I believe Celyse had one in her pocket when she left here. And if I'm right about that, I am confident that Celyse and Julio would have hidden it in the human realm."

I did a double take as all eyes shifted my way. "Um, what?"

"Do you know anything about a blue rock?" Uncle Leto asked me. "Or recall seeing one?"

I pictured my house—crisp white walls, dark wood floors, hues of green and blue decor sprinkled throughout. We had a lot of books and vases, and plenty of artwork, but I didn't recall seeing any blue rock.

"No, I don't think so. At least, I've never seen a blue rock in our house."

Leto folded his arms and continued pacing the library. "It would help greatly if we had some aquoise," he said. "There is no doubt about that. But what are the chances of Celyse and Julio having any?"

"We cannot ask them, since they are still missing," Lady Sonia added.

A spark of guilt twinged inside of me because I hadn't mentioned seeing my dad. After his confirmation that there was a traitor in Strong Haven, it could be someone in this very room. The less I said, the better.

"I say we go to the human realm and look," Leaf said.

"Go to my house?" My pulse quickened. Going back there could bring trouble. No way could I do that to my *abuela*. "I don't think so."

Uncle Leto's brow furrowed, and Lady Sonia's head turned sharply toward Leaf. The air in the room thickened, heavy with the danger in his suggestion.

"We must go," Leaf said. "It should not take long to look around." He held his hands together on top of the table. "It might be our only hope."

My brain processed our options. As far as I could tell, there were only two. Stay and be attacked and killed by a fae army, or go to my house and look for a stone that might help us.

"If that stone is the only thing that can help, then fine," I said, giving in. "Let's look. But we have to be fast, in and out."

Uncle Leto rubbed his face. He moving over to the window and looked out at the Strong Haven gardens. The day was perfect, and I wondered if their sun, moon, and stars knew an army of four provinces prepared to march down on us.

Finally, Leto turned our way. "The plan is set. Lady Sonia and I will stay and prepare Strong Haven. Gabriela and Leaf will go to her home in the human realm and search for the stone."

I stood quickly. "Leaf should stay here," I blurted. "To help prepare. I can take another guard."

"Absolutely not!" Leto barked. "Leaf is the most skilled warrior in all of Faevenly. And as skilled a fighter as you think you are, you are no match for a proper fae, let alone a soul vamp witch like Draven. Besides, the other provinces may have declared war against us, but it will take them time to assemble and travel to our doorstep. There is nothing we need Leaf for."

I knew he we was right, but I dreaded being with Leaf after our conversation in the garden. But at least I knew we wouldn't be alone. *Abuela* would be there. And Manny.

"Fine," I said reluctantly. "When do we leave?"

"Now," Leto said.

I blinked. "Now now?"

"Yes, now. Time is of the essence."

Lady Sonia and Uncle Leto made their way to the center of the study near a row of open windows. I pushed myself away from the table and rose to my feet. Leaf got up too, and we joined them.

The breeze from outside sifted through my hair, carrying with it the glorious aroma of a fresh bouquet of flowers. And for a few seconds, everything was normal. As if there were no enemy gathering against us, no traitor in our midst, no deadly witch on the loose. We were just hanging out in the study.

I would have much preferred being in Faevenly under different circumstances.

Leaf wore his stick slung on his back, along with a bow and a quiver of arrows. A dagger hung at his waist. I was glad he was armed, but sincerely hoped he wouldn't need all those weapons.

Lady Sonia stepped forward. "Do you need to retrieve anything before you go?"

Since I didn't bring anything with me, there was nothing for me to retrieve. I already had the one thing I wanted to keep, the stick slung at my back. "I have everything I need."

She handed me the small shimmery portal I had used earlier. "Collapse this from the other side so you can use it to come back when you are finished searching. We will see you when you return."

"Yes, we will see you," Uncle Leto said with a firm nod. "May you find what you seek."

I stretched out the thin, warm, and hazy portal. I lowered my hands as my kitchen came into view and a sea of emotions swept over me—joy to see my home, relief that my house looked okay, and an eagerness to see my *abuela*.

Taking swift steps, I crossed through, and Leaf followed. I gave Uncle Leto and Lady Sonia one last look, then placed my hands on the edges of the vapor and closed the portal until it was small enough to fit in my pocket. Slipping it away, I studied the empty kitchen. *Abuela* should've been here, cooking away her worries. But she wasn't. The counters were clean and the stovetop bare, though I detected the distinct aroma of cumin in the air.

I reached for the stick at my back. I laced my fingers around the wood and pulled it out nice and slow. Leaf furrowed his brow. He scanned the room and drew out his dagger.

"What is it?" he asked.

"My *abuela* should be here."

Taking slow steps, I started making my way to the living room but stopped when the back door opened. I spun around with my stick at the ready and saw *Abuela*. She screamed, dropping her bag of groceries.

Clutching her chest she exclaimed, "*¡Ay, Dios mio! ¡Me asustaste!*"

Leaf sheathed his weapon and started gathering the tomatoes, garlic, and onion that had rolled out on the floor while I went to her and hugged her. "I'm sorry, *Abuela*. I didn't mean to scare you."

She patted my back. "I'm so glad it was you. I've been so worried."

I bent down and picked up her bag of groceries and placed it on the counter. Leaf set the things he had gathered next to it, then walked over to shut the back door. He stayed there, stationed in his usual guard position.

"*¿Tu mamá y papá?*" she asked with a hopeful look on her face.

I wanted to tell her how I had seen my dad and what he had said, but not in front of Leaf. So instead, I shook my head and muttered. "They haven't been found. But I'm here to look for something they may have brought home years ago. Something that could help Faevenly and them too."

"Oh? What is it?" she asked.

"A blue stone called aquoise. It makes the user strong, and Uncle Leto and his forces need it."

She stitched her brows together. "*¿Porque, mija?* What is going on in Faevenly?"

Resisting the urge to glance at Leaf, I said, "All the other provinces except for one have declared war against Strong Haven."

She sucked in a breath and made the sign of the cross, lowering herself slowly onto a nearby stool. "*Ay, no.*"

"*Ay, sí,*" I said, making the sign of the cross too. "Things are pretty desperate, and that stone is really important."

Always ready to spring into action, she didn't stay seated long before she rolled up her sleeves and rose to her feet. "Well, then, let's get looking. We can search room by room starting upstairs and then working our way down."

With a nod, I followed *Abuela* up the stairs, and Leaf trailed behind us.

"I will look in the bathroom," *Abuela* said. "It shouldn't take me long."

"Okay," I replied. "Leaf and I can start in my room."

He followed me into my room and I hid a silent gulp. I hadn't really had a guy in my room before. Let alone someone like Leaf. He must've sensed my reservations because he maintained his impeccable manners.

"Where would you like me to start?" he asked.

Glancing over my things, I pointed at my bookshelf. "You can start there, and I'll start in my closet."

Clothes, shoes, and boxes filled with scarves, hats, and gloves crammed my small walk-in closet. I began dragging the boxes out and noticed Leaf leaning forward and looking at the pictures hanging on my wall. He pointed at one of me at a fencing tournament.

"You are a trained fighter?" he asked.

"I am. My mom raised me to fight like a fae, and I'm also on a fencing team at my school. I can wield a sword, a dagger, and a stick. I can even shoot a bow and arrow. And I'm pretty good with hand-to-hand combat."

"You said you were able to fight; now I understand." He considered me with a curious look. "As a human living in the human realm, why are you so highly trained?"

"Human with fae blood," I corrected, dumping out a box of purses. "My mom and dad wanted me to be able to defend myself. They said it was the fae way."

"They are not wrong about that being the fae way," he said.

He kept his gaze on the pictures, studying each one with heightened scrutiny. He stopped and zeroed in on one. I left my stuff on the floor and walked over to him.

"What is it?" I asked.

Following his line of sight, I moved my hand

toward the picture at the same time as him, our fingers grazing slightly. "My apologies," he said, dropping his hand quickly and stepping back.

Being close to him and touching him sent a burst of desire through me, but I pushed it away and focused on the picture. I was twelve and I was at my parents' bakery, sitting at a table in the office doing homework.

"That's me at my parents' bakery," I said. "I used to hang out there after school when they worked late."

"Look at the necklace you are wearing," he directed, indicating with his finger.

Moving closer to the picture, I studied my neckline and there it was. A silver chain with a cross and a blue stone. "What?" I whispered, my hand reaching for the cross around my neck. "That's the same chain I have on now with my cross, but I've never seen that blue stone before. Is that aquoise?"

Leaf motioned to the picture. "May I?"

"Yes," I said.

He took the picture from the wall and brought it closer. "That is aquoise, all right. Do you remember wearing it?"

"The chain and cross, yes. But not the stone." A chill prickled the back of my neck as I stared at the photo. Why didn't I remember that?

Abuela entered the room. "Did you find something?"

Leaf handed the picture to me and I passed it over to *Abuela*. "Look, it's the chain I'm wearing now, but there's an aquoise stone on it."

Her brow furrowed as she studied the stone. "I vaguely recall that you used to wear a blue stone with your cross." She scratched her forehead. "But I don't remember when you stopped."

"I don't remember it at all." The admission left a strange hollowness in my chest, like a gap where a memory should've been.

Leaf pointed at the picture. "This proves that the aquoise is here. Let us continue searching."

We tore through my room first, then the rest of the house. We checked drawers, closets, even under loose floorboards, but every corner came up empty. Each unsuccessful search only tightened the knot of frustration growing inside me.

"Now what?" I asked, feeling defeated as we gathered around the kitchen table, studying the picture of me wearing the stone.

"We go to this place," Leaf said, pointing at the picture. "The stone might still be there."

"Of course, the bakery," I answered. "My parents spend a lot of time there, and I did too when I was younger. So I guess it could be there somewhere."

Abuela grabbed her purse and her keys. "*Vamos.*"

I wanted to match her enthusiasm, but before I could get to that state, I raised my finger and said, "Give me two minutes so I can change out of this dress."

"Okay," she replied. "But hurry."

I made a move for the hallway, and so did Leaf. I

stopped in my tracks and turned around. "Um, I don't need you to come with me to change my clothes."

"Lord Letormis asked me to keep you close. So I will keep you close."

I flashed *Abuela* a raised brow, hoping for some back up, but she shrugged her shoulders. "Not inside your room," she said. "But if he is close by to protect you, then I am okay with that. He can wait outside in the hallway."

"Fine," I blew out.

Making my way up the stairs, I thought it ironic how he had asked me to stay away from him and then Uncle Leto had asked him to stay close. The idea of it made me chuckle.

"This amuses you?" Leaf asked from behind me.

I got to my door and turned to face him. "It does. I find it funny how you didn't want to be close to me, and now you are *ordered* to be close."

He placed his hands behind his back as he took one more step toward me, maintaining his stoic expression. "I never said I did not want to be close to you."

Heat rushed my cheeks and my heart sped up. I wasn't expecting him to say that.

He backed away to the wall, then motioned with his hand. "Go ahead. I will be right here." He looked at me like he wanted to say more but didn't.

"Um, okay," I whispered.

I went in and shut the door and stood against the wood for a few seconds. So he wanted to be close to me, but sometimes he acted like he didn't. I was more confused than ever. But I couldn't think about him right now. I needed to focus.

With a shake of my head, I stripped out of my dress and slipped on a pair of jeans and a fitted purple t-shirt. Then I switched out the dainty slippers for my brown boots.

Staring at myself in the mirror, I touched my cross with my fingertips, studying my long black hair with white streaks that was still braided in the front and tied in the back. I touched the curve of my outer ear, following the ridge with my fingertips. Mom's ears were only slightly pointed, and mine weren't pointed at all.

But I was still a fae.

"I am the proud daughter of a fae princess and a human witch," I whispered to myself. "And everything I am as a fae and a witch will help me." And then, I added for good measure while making the sign of the cross, "Please. Amen."

When I exited my room, I found Leaf in his regular leaning position. He studied me with intensity, sending a warm flush throughout my body. "I'm ready," I said, looking away from him quickly.

He fell in step behind me as I went downstairs and into the kitchen. *Abuela* had her colorful purse slung over her shoulder and her keys in hand. She held them out to me, and I took them.

"You drive, *mija*. I already called Manny and told him we were coming."

"He got back from his conference okay?"

"He did and he's been worried sick about you. He'll be glad that you're back."

Her mentioning calling Manny made me think about my phone. I had left it upstairs in my room when I stepped into Faevenly, and hadn't touched it since. I was sure Aliana had been texting me like crazy.

Hopping into the car, *Abuela* sat beside me and Leaf sat in the back. Rolling out of the driveway, I glanced at *Abuela*. "Have you heard from Aliana?"

"*¡Oh, sí!* She came by to check on you and I told her you went to Faevenly to help your parents. I forgot to tell you, *mija. Lo siento.*"

"That's okay. I'm glad you told her so she wouldn't worry about me." Though, of course, I knew Aliana was totally worrying because that was her thing. She worried about everything.

We fell into silence as drive out of my lakeside subdivision and to the highway that led to the bakery. After a fifteen-minute drive, I pulled into the parking lot, noticing right away how empty the usually packed lot was. Examining the glass windows, I saw the lights were dimmed and the red CLOSED sign was lit. Uncle Manny stood by the back employee entrance. He rushed over to open *Abuela's* door.

He helped her out, hugged her, then wrapped me up in his arms and held on. "Boy am I relieved to see you. Everything okay with you?" He stepped back and began patting my shoulders and arms. "No injuries?"

"I'm fine."

He raised his brow at Leaf while studying his face. "But I see you were in a fight. What happened?"

"I killed Alexander Kane."

Uncle Manny's eyebrows shot up. "Whoa, what?"

Leaf kept silent and didn't explain anything about how it happened, but Uncle Manny didn't seem to care.

He lowered his brows, then said, "Well, it's about damn time." Then he turned his attention to me. "Any word on your parents?"

"Not yet," I answered.

I wanted to tell Uncle Manny and Abuela about seeing my dad, but his warning to keep it secret stopped me. Although I trusted Leaf, I couldn't be completely sure.

"Come in," Uncle Manny said. "I closed the shop so we wouldn't be disturbed. So it's just us."

He led us inside, where the aroma of bread, cinnamon, vanilla, and spice permeated the air. Baking dishes and bowls of all sizes lined the shelves on one side. On the other were large clear canisters of ingredients like flour, sugar, cinnamon, and herbs along with fun toppings like sprinkles, chocolate shavings, and marshmallows. There were three industrial-sized ovens, a couple of refrigerators, and several mixers and waffle makers.

Off to the side was a door marked *OFFICE*, and we filed in one by one. The lavender-painted room had a table, two desks, a sink, a refrigerator, and a row of cabinets. I sat slowly, fresh pain gripping my heart, my mind taking me back to all the time I'd spent here when I was little helping my mom and dad with whatever they needed.

Now, I was here again, needing to help them and Faevenly.

Uncle Manny pulled out a chair for *Abuela*, but the rest of us stayed standing. He rubbed his hands through his thick hair. "*Abuela* said on the phone that war is coming to Strong Haven? And y'all are looking for aquoise?" He looked from me to Leaf. "Is that right?"

"It is, and we are," Leaf said. "All the provinces, except the Sublands, have turned against us. We're outnumbered and desperate for an advantage. I remembered Celyse had a piece of aquoise in her pocket when she came through the Sublands tunnels, and I thought we might find it here. Lord Letormis sent Gabriela and me to recover it and we found a picture of her in the bakery wearing the stone on her chain when she was younger."

A visible shiver raced through Manny as fear danced in his eyes. "The tunnels," he whispered, looking terrified. "After all these years, that experience has never left me."

"Nor I," Leaf added. He reached out and placed his hand on Manny's shoulder. "But that was long ago. The tunnels do not exist anymore. Neither does the aquoise, at least not in the fae realm. That is why we are here."

"We need to find it, Uncle Manny," I added. "Before Strong Haven is attacked. It may be our only hope."

Manny rubbed his face. "Okay, yeah. Let's start looking, then."

We moved around the office opening drawers and cabinets, rifling through every file folder and closed container, but found nothing.

"Let's look out in the kitchen," Manny said.

We stepped out of the office, and for the first time I noticed just how many jars and containers of various sizes filled up the space. Not to mention the huge pantry, the walk-in freezer, and all the drawers and cabinets.

"We should split up," I said, considering the impossible task.

"Good idea," Uncle Manny agreed. He motioned to the right side of the room. "Leaf and I will start over there. You and *Abuela* take the other side."

Although part of me wanted to team up with Leaf, I was glad to be working with *Abuela*. If we could move far enough across the room, I could whisper to her how I had seen my dad. I'd have to be super careful though, so Leaf didn't hear.

We opened a tall white cabinet. Glass containers of different sizes were stacked from top to bottom. "That's a lot of glass," I groaned.

"We will work fast, *mija*. I'll start at the bottom," she said, crouching down to her knees. "You can take the top."

Glancing over my shoulder, I found Leaf and

Manny busy inside the pantry. I quickly kneeled down and whispered as low as I could against her ear. "I saw Dad."

Her mouth fell open, but I pressed my finger to my lips, then flicked my eyes in the direction of Uncle Manny and Leaf. She closed her mouth, then scooted closer.

"He whisked my mind to where he and Mom were. He said they're okay. Then he told me there's a traitor in Faevenly."

Her eyes widened, nearly popping out of her head. Returning to a normal size, her gaze darted to the pantry. "You think it's Leaf?"

I shook my head. "I don't think so. He was here in the human realm when Draven escaped, plus he's saved me a few times." *And kissed me.* "But I suppose it could be him. Or Lady Sonia or Uncle Leto. There's also a guy named Dain who's the head of security. If anyone had an opportunity to free Draven, it'd be him."

Leaf and Uncle Manny emerged from the pantry and started on a set of cabinets. I casually moved away from *Abuela* and reached up for a glass container when a low vibration filled my ears. It spread through me like a thousand pinpricks, gathering at the back of my neck. *Abuela* slammed her hand on my arm, undoubtedly feeling it too.

"*Mija*," she said with alarm.

Leaf dashed in front of me, his dagger out. "What is it?"

Manny hustled over. "What's happening?"

Before I could answer, the back door ripped away with a metal snap, rocking the bakery like a bomb, and a tall figure dressed in all black with a hooded cloak walked in. A hint of red mist hovered around him like a deadly fog.

"Draven," Leaf hissed.

My gut twisted tight. *Oh no… Draven?*

"Hello, Leaf," the witch said in a silky smooth voice. The kind that was intoxicating and mesmerizing, as if he were a supercharged hypnotist. "And hello Gabriela, daughter of Strong Haven. Offspring of fae princess Celyse and human witch Julio. I have been *most* eager to make your acquaintance."

He moved toward us, his hood shrouding his face in shadow. He took slow and graceful steps, like a panther stalking a mouse, his cloak drifting behind him with each movement. With each step he made, *Abuela* and I made slow steps back.

Leaf raised his dagger. "Stay where you are."

Draven stopped. He lowered his hood, as if ready to perform on some magic stage, revealing shiny jet-black hair braided at the sides while the rest flowed down his back. His skin was porcelain white, and his eyes sparkled like dazzling diamonds. Dramatically pointed ears poked through his hair, and his thin lips were the perfect shade of red. I wasn't expecting him to look so young and striking.

"I will do what I want. You should know that by now, Leaf Kane of the Sublands."

I drew in a sharp breath, my mind reeling. I glanced at Leaf. *Kane, as in the Kanes from High Meadow*?

"I do not claim that name," he hissed through clenched teeth. "It does not belong to me."

"Claim it or not, it is part of your bloodline. Is it not?"

Instead of waiting for a response from Leaf, Draven's gaze zeroed in on me and his lips tugged into a wicked smile. "I take it from your reaction you did not know that you are keeping company with a dreaded Kane?"

I had no response; I was too shocked.

Leaf kept his dagger out, his grip tight around the blade. "What do you want?"

The red hue around Draven darkened and expanded as he licked his lips. "I want this daughter. Her body, her soul, her heart in my hands. It is long overdue to me."

Abuela's grip on my arm jerked, then dropped. I glanced back to check on her and found her slumping to the floor, her hands clutching her chest. I crashed to my knees beside her and cradled her head from the fall. Her brow furrowed and a pained grimace spread across her face. Uncle Manny slid beside me.

"¡*Abuela!*" I cried.

She managed a smile, her expression mixed with love and sadness. She nodded at Manny then looked at me. "*Eres una mujer poderosa*," she whispered. "A blessed child of God, filled with great power."

Her body went slack, her eyes dimmed, and her hands fell to her sides. Disbelief and anger rocked me, sending shivers through my body.

Manny gulped. "*¿Abuela?*"

"Fragile, pathetic, human," Draven snarled. "Dead on her own without any intervention from me."

Gently easing my hands out from under *Abuela's* head, I looked up at him, then slowly rose to my feet. "You're a monster."

"Oh yes, I am most certainly a monster. And now it is time for the monster to perform." He stretched his arms out to either side and gave me a mocking bow. "Are you ready to die, Gabriela, daughter of Strong Haven?"

Are you ready to die? My heart skipped a beat. It was the same question Uncle Leto asked each time we fought. Were our fights preparing me for this? Did he know this would happen to me?

I unsheathed the stick at my back, mustering all my strength, refusing to be scared. "No," I said as I tilted my head to one side. "Are you?"

He narrowed his gaze at me, but before either one of us could make a move, Leaf hurled his dagger. Manny threw a glass bowl. With a growl, Draven flung out his hand, unleashing a blinding blast of red light. The radiance exploded around me, sending crackling sparks of energy every which way.

Light. Like my dad and *abuela* had said. Was this Draven's aura? Was this what my dad could do... what I could do?

I focused on my hands and moved to raise them, but couldn't. I was frozen. My entire body stuck. Flicking my eyes about, I spotted Leaf's dagger and Uncle Manny's bowl suspended in midair. They were frozen too.

Draven moved in. He brought his face close to mine, sending the intoxicating aroma of musk and cloves and cedar swirling around me while his dazzling eyes held me in a trance. "Be a good little princess and stay here while I take care of the others. I am saving you for last."

I wanted to scream at him, wanted to attack, but I couldn't. I was powerless.

He moved towards Leaf's dagger, his steps slow and calculated. He ran his long thin finger across the blade, then plucked it from the air. He twirled it in his hand as he approached Uncle Manny and Leaf.

He was going to kill them.

Fear surged inside of me. Panic took over my senses. My mind screamed out, shrieking for Draven to go away. My body quaked and my brain zapped and a surge of purple light flooded my vision before everything went black.

CHAPTER 18

Soft movement soothed me, strong arms cradled me close, and an overwhelming sense of safety nestled in my heart. My eyes fluttered open and I saw the most beautiful face with a perfectly chiseled jaw, elegantly pointed nose, high cheekbones, and full lips. A soft light radiated from behind.

"Are you an angel?" I whispered.

Sparkling blue eyes looked down on me. "No, little princess. I am no angel."

Mesmerized by the gorgeous face, I blinked as images slowly flashed before my eyes until a deluge of memories flooded my brain. The bakery... Draven... my *abuela*... Uncle Manny... Leaf...

Snapping to my senses, I realized I was in Leaf's arms, his stride steady and sure as he carried me through my house. My head throbbed, and the scent of smoke and metal clung to his clothes. My hands trembled against his chest, the lingering buzz of power still pulsing beneath my skin.

My eyes widened with alarm. "Leaf, what happened? Did I—" My voice faltered as flashes of the bakery, the heat, the light, slammed into me. "What did I do?"

His grip tightened slightly. "Shhh, everything is okay now," he soothed, his voice low and calm. He continued down the hallway and up the stairs, his hold on me unyielding but gentle. "You called forth your power and expelled Draven from the bakery."

"I did?" The words came out barely above a whisper. My mind reeled, trying to connect the flashes of light and heat to my own hands. The memory felt distant, unreal—like watching someone else inside me lose control.

He opened my door and stepped inside, the faintest hint of a smile touching his lips. "You did." His gaze lingered on me—not with judgment, but with something that almost looked like pride. "You bested Draven, Gabriela. You should rest now."

I remembered my desperate anger when Draven plucked Leaf's dagger from the air, but couldn't remember anything after.

"How did we get here? Where's my Uncle Manny?" I swallowed hard, tears stinging my eyes as the image of *Abuela's* lifeless form filled my mind. My voice became so small. "And my *abuela*?"

He laid me gently on my bed. "Whatever you did brought her back from the edge of death and Manny went with her to the hospital in an ambulance."

"She's alive?" I sat up with a jerk. The sudden movement made the room spin and my head pound with pain, and I winced.

"Careful there," he said, helping to ease me back down. "She is alive, and she will be fine."

My panic was far from over, though. "What about Draven? Where is he?" I whispered, as if saying his name out loud would send some sort of signal to him.

"I do not know where he is. But before your grandmother was placed in the ambulance, she told me to bring you here. She said this place is warded and no evil can enter."

"Oh," I muttered, adding the fact that my house was warded to the long list of things I knew nothing about.

"Do not worry. I will be right here with you." He lowered himself onto the edge of my bed and held my hand.

I was about to thank him when Draven's words that Leaf was a Kane came crashing down on me. "You're a Kane," I uttered.

My eyes studied him, recognizing how much he looked like Alexander. They had the same jet-black hair, same tall and slender build, and same piercing blue eyes. The only real difference between them was that Leaf had full lips and Alexander had thin ones.

"Why didn't you tell me?" I asked. The words came out softer than I intended, caught somewhere between accusation and disbelief. Part of me felt betrayed, the other part afraid of the answer.

He stayed on the edge of the bed but released my hand and angled his body away from me. He looked down at the floor. "There is nothing to tell. I claim neither their name nor their bloodline, and they do not claim me."

I gently propped myself up, watching the tension in his shoulders. "But why? What happened?" The question slipped out before I could stop it. I needed to understand—to bridge the distance between us that suddenly grew wider than ever.

He maintained his expressionless and stoic demeanor and clasped his hands together. "I was born out of wedlock when the elder Lord Kane bedded a human. After my birth, she was killed and I was cast out and exiled to the Sublands. At the time, that's where the lowest dredges and half-bred fae were sent. Rook and his family took me in and raised me."

My lips parted as my mind processed that Leaf was part human. Like me. And that his mother was killed, and he wasn't wanted and was sent away. My heart broke for him, and finally I was able to understand the pain and hurt he'd been carrying around.

I reached out and touched his hand. "I'm so sorry, Leaf."

He rose to his feet and my hand fell from him. "I neither want nor need your pity," he said in a biting tone.

I stayed like that, looking at him as if I had never seen the true him before. And wondering if I was seeing it now. He was so confusing. When he carried me into my room and placed me on my bed, I could feel his warmth and tenderness. But now, the part of him that was wounded and pained had reared its head again.

I shook my head, frustration tightening in my chest. "I wish I could understand you."

He didn't answer right away. His gaze lingered for a moment before he spoke. "That is something no one should wish for." He walked to the door, pausing with his hand on the frame before glancing back at me. "You should rest. I will be outside in the corridor."

"Stop," I called out, sitting up all the way despite the throbbing pain.

He stayed where he was and held his silence.

"I wish it, Leaf." I clutched my hand and pressed it against my chest. "I want to know you. Really and truly know you. The good and the bad, all of it. I don't scare easily and I'm not one to run away when things get hard or complicated." I eased myself off my bed and walked over to him, taking his hands in mine. "Please, Leaf. Will you let me in?"

He slowly pulled his hands away. "I cannot. I am damaged. I am ruined. I am wretched and lost. There is no hope for me. None. And if you know what is good for you, you will stay away from me."

With one last look at me, he left my room and closed the door with a soft click.

———

THE NIGHT WAS LONG AND I COULDN'T SLEEP. I TOSSED and turned while my thoughts raced. They were filled with my ever-increasing fear about Draven. I pictured the smooth-talking, mesmerizing witch lurking somewhere outside, waiting for me to venture out of my house and step over our wards so he could destroy me.

But more than that, I couldn't stop thinking about Leaf.

Feeling physically miserable and emotionally drained, I thought water and an ibuprofen might help. I got up, tiptoed across my wood floor and slowly opened my door. When I stepped out, Leaf wasn't there.

Panic flooded me and my stomach tightened. Where was he? I stayed perfectly still, holding my breath, listening for the slightest sound that might tell me where he had gone. But all I heard was a breezy wind outside and the tinkling of wind chimes. I stepped back into my room to get a weapon and realized I had no idea what had happened to the stick Leaf had given me. My eyes darted around my room, looking for something I could use in its place, when they landed on my bookshelf filled with fencing trophies. I crept over, carefully avoiding the place where my wood floor always squeaked, and got the tallest one. I held it out as I stepped back into the hallway.

The irony of a girl needing a weapon was not lost on the fact that the top of my trophy was a girl with a weapon.

"Appropriate," I muttered.

With slow and careful movements, I crept to the

stairs and carefully made my way down to the foyer. I stood still, straining my ears, but didn't hear anything. I eased my way up to the front door. Pressing up against the wood, I looked out the peephole. The soft glow from our landscaping lighting revealed trees, bushes, and grass.

But no sign of Leaf.

My hands grew sweaty, and my heart thrummed against my chest as I crept down the hallway, past the living room, and to the kitchen, holding my breath deep in my chest. Stopping at the kitchen table, I stayed perfectly motionless as I scanned the area around me.

"Gabriela?"

I spun around, trophy raised, grip tightened, and saw Leaf. "Leaf!" I set the trophy on the table and leaned over, catching my breath. "You scared the hell out of me."

He eyed my choice of weapon. "I did not mean to. My apologies."

With my breathing returning to normal, I asked, "Where were you?"

"I was outside, doing a perimeter check. I did not expect you to awaken."

"In order for me to have awakened, I would've needed to have first gone to sleep. So it's okay."

He tilted his head. "You have been awake this entire time?"

"Yes, but not by choice. I couldn't fall asleep after our..." I was going to let my words trail off because I didn't want him to know how bothered I was at being rejected by him, but I pushed out that last word anyway. "... talk." I cleared my throat and avoided his gaze before continuing on. "That and my concern for my *abuela*. I thought water and something for my headache would do me good."

I walked over to the cabinet where Mom kept different medicines and herbs. The smells of chamomile, echinacea, and ginger wafted out, reminding me of how worried I was for her and my dad. Pushing those fears aside, I found a bottle of ibuprofen and fished out one of the pills. I took out a glass and filled it with water from our refrigerator.

Keeping an eye on Leaf who stayed close to the wall, I remembered how *Abuela* had wanted me to offer him some *caldo*. Her lesson of generosity prompted me to think he might want some water too. So I got a glass for him and filled it up.

"Here you go," I said, extending it out for him.

"Thank you," he said, taking it and moving away from me quickly. Getting his message loud and clear, I couldn't get away from him fast enough.

"I'm going back to my room now."

Walking at a quick pace, I hurried back upstairs. In the hallway before I opened my door, he spoke.

"Gabriela."

His emotion-filled voice stilled me, and it took me a few long seconds to turn around.

He took my glass of water and set both his and mine on the floor. He leaned in. His scent, his closeness, the way his eyes seemed to drink me in, his mood and intensity—it all sent me soaring.

"Yes?" My voice came out barely above a whisper, my pulse hammering in my throat.

He placed his hands up against the wall behind me, as if claiming me as his. "I do not want you to stay away from me."

My breath hitched. Heat rushed through me, scattering my thoughts. I could feel the strength in his arms, the faint tremor in his exhale, the space between us charged and trembling. Every nerve in my body screamed to close the distance, to surrender to whatever this was. "I don't want you to stay away from me," I whispered, the words leaving me before I could think.

He pressed his forehead against mine and brought his hand up to my neck, letting his fingers trail down to the hollow of my throat. My skin was on fire everywhere he touched.

"I cannot fight you anymore."

"Then don't," I breathed. "Don't fight what you feel for me."

He kept his gaze on mine, as if searching my very soul. Then, with a tilt of his head, he kissed me. His soft lips sent my head into the clouds as our tongues explored each other's mouths softly at first, then turning desperate and wild.

Wanting him completely, I pulled him to me as I pressed myself against his hard body, eliminating any space between us, needing to feel all of him.

"Leaf," I moaned, blissfully getting lost in him as his lips made their way to my neck. "Oh, Leaf."

He backed up and studied me with tender longing, then lifted me up with such grace I hardly knew my feet left the ground. I wrapped my legs around his waist as he flung open the door and carried me in. We crashed down on my bed, our lips connecting again and again and again.

He paused, his chest heaving, as he drew back and looked down on me with his seductive blue eyes. "You are so beautiful."

Fiery impulses for him roared inside of me while I reached out and caressed his perfect face, tracing his chiseled jaw with my fingertips, careful to avoid his cuts and bruises. "You're the one who's beautiful."

He kept his gaze on me for a few long seconds before lowering himself down on me again, wrapping his arms around me and kissing me so completely I was soaring.

"Take me, Leaf," I whispered against his mouth.

"I will devour you if you let me," he growled softy, while his hands explored my body, sending waves of desire pulsating through me.

"Then devour me," I panted.

Nothing else existed that night but us. Not our dire circumstances, nor our uncertain future. It was just me and him and fire and passion as we gave each other everything.

CHAPTER 19

Soft knocking on my door woke me up. Sitting up with a panic-filled jerk, I was reaching for the blanket at the foot of my bed when I realized Leaf wasn't with me. He was gone, and I was wearing a long T-shirt and pajama pants.

"Gabriela, it's Uncle Manny." He knocked again, a little louder. "Can I come in?"

I sucked in a sharp breath, then glanced at my clock. It was six in the morning. Leaf must've heard Uncle Manny drive up and dressed me before leaving the room.

I reached over and turned on my lamp, then smoothed my hair down, threading it behind my ears. "Uh, yes, come in."

He opened the door. Dark, puffy circles outlined his bloodshot eyes, and I didn't think he'd slept at all. "Hey, *mija*." He walked over to me.

"Hey, Uncle Manny. How's *Abuela*?" The words caught in my throat. Worry twisted in my stomach, followed quickly by guilt. While they'd spent the night in the hospital, I'd been wrapped up in Leaf—forgetting what really mattered.

"She had a heart attack, but she's going to be okay." He rubbed my leg in that reassuring way. "She had a stent put in last night and she's resting well."

"Thank goodness she's going to be okay," I muttered, touching the cross around my neck.

"Thank goodness is right. She's even back to ordering me around." He smiled. "Sent me to get a few things she had packed in her suitcase. She also said she wants you to stay here with Leaf and not go anywhere."

"Don't worry. I'm not going anywhere. When do you think she'll be released?" I asked, knowing how much she probably hated being there, and also thinking I really needed her help with the aquoise.

"The doc said about twenty-four hours." Another pat on my leg. "Knowing her, maybe sooner."

"Oh," I uttered, thinking we couldn't wait that long to look for the stone, and wondering what we could do without her.

Uncle Manny folded his arms and changed the subject. "Gabriela, do you remember what you did in the bakery with Draven? With your aura? Your light?"

"Remember? Not really," I admitted, trying to recall the details but unable to do so. I only remembered the fear and the pressure inside of me building until it broke free, and then nothing but light.

He pulled out my desk chair and sat, folding his hands together on his lap. "Do you know *how* you were able to do what you did?"

"No," I answered, shaking my head. "I've picked

apart the scene in my brain, and I have no idea how I did what I did."

Uncle Manny took on a faraway look. "Your dad didn't understand it either, or know how to control it. In fact, your Uncle Leto tried to get your dad to summon his gifts by shooting arrows at his head."

"Uncle Leto did what?"

Manny chuckled. "The arrows never actually hit him. Well, I mean, they did, but only a little bit. At the end of Leto's session, your dad was nicked up pretty bad. He had small cuts and blood everywhere. I kept thinking how pissed off *Abuela* was going to be when she saw him."

I pictured Uncle Leto firing arrows at my dad's head and shuddered. I most certainly didn't want to go through an exercise like that. "Did the arrow thing work? Was my dad able to make himself use his powers?"

Uncle Manny shook his head. "Nope, it never worked. But when your dad needed to use his gifts"— Uncle Manny pushed his hands out—"it just came out of him."

I stared down at my own hands. "Do you think I'll be able to do the same thing?"

He flashed me a reassuring smile. "Of course I do. Like father, like daughter, right? Plus, since you did it once, you can do it again. I have no doubt."

The logic made sense to me, and I was desperate to hold on to some sort of hope. "What about the aquoise?"

Uncle Manny's positive expression dashed away. "I don't know. My only suggestion is to keep looking around here and that maybe *Abuela* can figure something out when she gets released." He rose to his feet. "But for now, I need to get her things and get going."

He left to get *Abuela's* stuff, and I stepped out of my room to join him, meeting Leaf's gaze. He was fully dressed, standing at alert in the hallway, looking incredible.

"Good morning," I said, trying to sound completely normal.

"Good morning," replied.

I went straight to the guest room where Uncle Manny was gathering *Abuela's* things. She didn't have a lot of stuff, so packing up only took a few minutes. With the duffel bag zipped and draped over his shoulder, he kissed my cheek and hugged me.

"Stay close to Leaf," I said. "I'll be back later tonight, and if all goes well with *Abuela*, she'll be back tomorrow."

As quick as he showed up, he was quicker to leave. And I was alone again with Leaf. But now, everything had changed between us. I had shared my body and passion with him, an act I considered the most intimate physical expression between two souls. An act I had never done before and did not take lightly. As much as I wanted to stay in that moment and experience him again, seeing Uncle Manny and hearing about *Abuela* in the hospital reminded me of our dire mission.

We needed to continue searching for the aquoise. My parents and all of Faevenly depended on me.

After a quick shower and a change of clothes, and spending a few extra minutes on my hair and makeup, I opened the door to find Leaf standing patiently in the hallway as usual. I wanted to throw my arms around him and kiss him, but he looked like he was back in duty mode, which is what I needed to be in too.

"We need to keep looking for the aquoise," he said.

"We do," I nodded in agreement. I walked up to him and placed my hands on his chest. "And when this is over and behind us, we can pick up where we left off."

He moved his hands to mine and slowly pulled them off his body. "The task ahead of us should remain our priority, Gabriela." A hint of sorrow mixed with regret crept across his face as he added, "We cannot know what will become of either of us when this is over."

What? I stifled a gulp, surprised at his words, but taking the hint loud and clear as I stepped back. We had truly connected and broken down those walls last night. Shared something special.

Maybe I was naive, but this felt like it could be forever—because he had my heart completely. Whatever was between us was so different from anything I had ever felt before.

But it wasn't the same for him. And I felt like an idiot.

"Yeah, you're right," I agreed, increasing the

distance between us and clearing my throat. "Who knows what will happen." And then I added quickly, "Um, excuse me for a quick second."

Walking back to the bathroom, I took slow and calm strides so he wouldn't know how badly he had hurt me. Once inside, I turned the faucet on high and gripped the edges of the white porcelain sink.

Tears welled up in my eyes and slipped out onto my cheeks, my heart cracking. The pain sharp and real. I had just given him *everything*, thinking it meant something, but his words told me otherwise. For him, it was nothing.

I scooped the water into my hands and splashed my face, telling myself it was fine. I was fine. He didn't mean anything to me. Our night together was nothing but a huge mistake. A distraction from our worlds falling apart around us. He was only a fae guard and I hardly knew him, and he obviously didn't know me.

I turned off the water, then tugged at the hand towel and dabbed my cheeks. Then I straightened my back and smoothed my long hair, pulling some strands of white behind my ears. Protecting my heart with an invisible shield, I resigned to finish what we had started and find the aquoise. I would focus on that alone.

Turning on the role of princess, I rejoined Leaf with my head held high. "Let's go downstairs and continue our search."

He quietly fell in step behind me as we made our way to the kitchen. When we got there, I realized how hungry I was, but I didn't want to take the time for a meal. The quicker I found the stone, the sooner I could help Faevenly, find my parents, say goodbye to Leaf, and get my life back.

I grabbed a granola bar from the pantry, opened it, and took a bite. I also got some water. This time, I didn't offer Leaf anything.

"What do you propose we do?" he asked, his voice careful, almost too calm. He shifted his weight, the faint scrape of his boots against the tile breaking the silence between us.

"We continue the search," I said, keeping my gaze fixed on the granola bar in my hand. "Not in the regular way, but the Avila way."

He moved closer, the air tightening around us, but I refused to look at him. My heart still ached from what he'd said, from what he *hadn't* said. I needed distance —needed control.

He moved a step closer, but I didn't look at him. "Are you referring to your abilities as a witch?"

I nodded once, still not meeting his eyes. "That's exactly what I mean." My voice came out steadier than I felt. "My abilities aren't anywhere near my dad's or my *abuela's*, but I can do things. We saw that in the bakery."

I took one last bite of my bar, sipped my water, then sat at the table.

"Where should I stand?" Leaf asked.

"As far away from me as possible," I said, hoping my words sounded as rude as I meant.

Sitting at the kitchen table, I pushed Leaf from my mind and remembered sitting here with my abuela, learning how to connect my mind to hers. It was a wild idea, but maybe I could do the same thing with the aquoise.

"What are you going to do?" Leaf asked, standing opposite from me and nearly out of the breakfast nook.

"My mind is going to be friends with the aquoise necklace I was wearing in the picture," I said, wishing he'd be quiet.

"Friends?" he asked.

"It's hard to explain; but yes, friends. And if you don't mind, I'd really appreciate it if you'd stop talking to me." Then I muttered under my breath, "Like, forever."

I blew out a breath, relaxing my body as best I could—until my thoughts zipped back to my night with Leaf. With an internal grunt, I pushed it away, forcing myself to focus, reminding myself he meant nothing to me.

"Aquoise," I said softly.

I closed my eyes and stilled myself, saying a silent prayer to God, his angels, and saints to watch over me. Turning my thoughts away from the house, from the kitchen, I concentrated on the photo of myself in the bakery.

At first, there was nothing. Just darkness and the steady rhythm of my breath. Then, faint and flickering, something stirred.

Not a voice. Not a thought. A feeling.

It pulsed softly against my mind—warm, distant, and unfamiliar—like it was waiting... or watching.

I pictured as many details as I could—the silver chain, the blue stone the size of a quarter, the lavender walls, the table cluttered with homework. I imagined myself so close to the stone I could see my current self reaching out to my younger self, as if I were really there. Or at least my mind was.

Everything zoomed into focus with perfect clarity. The sweet smell of waffles and muffins tickled my nose. The overhead light glinted across the shiny metallic file cabinets. I inched in and leaned closer to myself, marveling at how young and innocent I looked. Bringing my gaze to my necklace with the cross and the blue stone, I wondered where the stone had gone.

Where are you? I thought, trying to communicate with the stone, focusing on it alone. *Why aren't you with me anymore?*

Like a wave, a tingle coursed through my body as different scenes whisked before my eyes. My parents being attacked in the bakery. My younger self standing and watching as I grasped my necklace. An earth-shattering scream rocketing out of me. A purple blast consuming my sight.

My heart raced and my hands shook. Did those things really happen? And if they did, why couldn't I remember them?

Without warning, my vision dimmed, my body dropped, and my stomach tumbled as I soared through darkness in a wild free fall until I crashed face first against a hard grassy surface. A series of coughs burst out of me, along with tufts of grass and leaves. When my hacking stopped, I raised myself up on my forearms, finding myself in the middle of a lavender-filled meadow. I recognized the spot immediately.

"Dad?"

He blurred into view before me. "*Mija*, I'm here."

I lifted myself off the ground and rushed into his arms. He held me in a fierce grip and patted my back while tears spilled out of me. "Dad," I choked out.

"Shhh, my girl. My amazing, beautiful girl. Everything is going to be okay."

"I don't know," I muttered as the tears fell down my face. "I don't know anything anymore."

He held me close, rocking me side to side for a bit. Then he gently pulled back and looked at my face. "We may not have much time, so tell me what's going on."

My brain was cluttered with everything that had happened since he and mom went missing, but at that moment, I needed to know about what I had just seen. "Dad, were you and mom attacked in the bakery when I was little?"

His lips parted and he cast his eyes down, staring at the ground for a few seconds. He slowly brought his stare back to me. "Yes."

My breathing hitched and my hands trembled. "Was I there?"

He drew in a deep breath. "Yes."

"Dad," I finally spoke clearly, clutching his arms.

"Why don't I remember? And why didn't y'all ever talk about it?" I glanced around. "And where is Mom?"

"One thing at a time, *mija*," he said in a soft tone. "Okay?"

I nodded, then wiped my face, not understanding how I could cry and touch my face in this strange world or realm or whatever it was, but not caring. I needed my dad to explain.

"When your mom and I left Faevenly, we didn't think it would be without consequences. Your mother was a princess of Strong Haven after all, and Strong Haven was not without its fair share of enemies. One day, three fae who had been living in the human realm learned about your mother and I owning the bakery. So they paid us a not-so-friendly visit. You were there, in the office, and when you stepped out, they attacked." He moved in and took my hands. "You screamed so loud, your aura shot out of you like a sunburst. When your light dissipated, we saw that the three attackers were obliterated. All that was left of them was dust."

I sucked in a breath and held it deep inside as shock rippled through every inch of me. "I don't remember," I uttered.

"I know. Your mind either wiped it away or kept it hidden to protect you. Your mom and I wanted to protect you too. So we began distancing ourselves from the fae realm. We stopped talking about it and began visiting less and less until we didn't travel there anymore. We even put away all evidence of the realm from our home, including an aquoise charm you used to wear on that necklace with your cross. That's also when we started training you to defend yourself, in case anyone ever tried to attack you in the future. It was the only way to assure your safety."

My mind reeled and my hands shook. "I was feeling so bad about not knowing my fae heritage, but it wasn't me not caring. You and mom kept me away to keep me from harm."

His eyes filled with tears and he nodded. "We did, *mija*."

Everything I had ever known turned upside down, as if I didn't even know who I was anymore. A person with immense power, descended from a fae bloodline I didn't know because my parents had shielded me from it. Now that I had experienced some of the perils of Faevenly, I understood why.

I pulled my dad in for a hug, my heart breaking at seeing him so vulnerable. "I understand, Dad."

"I hope so," he muttered. "Your mother and I have only ever wanted to keep you safe."

"I know." My gaze swept the meadow. "But where is she? Where is Mom? Why isn't she—"

The soft stomping of hooves and the creak of wheels broke through the stillness. Turning, I caught sight of a lone and majestic silver Enbarr trotting across the field, pulling a cart draped in linen and shadow. Three figures lay upon it, bodies clothed in white.

My breath snagged. The world tilted. No—this couldn't be what I thought it was. Icy fear flooded me, as the faint shimmer of faelight hovered the field and the truth crashed over me like a tidal wave.

This was no ordinary place. No ordinary cart. It was the Passing Place. Where the fae went after death.

My knees wobbled, and a sound escaped me—half gasp, half sob—as cold recognition settled in my bones. *They're gone.* My parents were here. My mom. My dad.

"Dad." The word cracked, raw and broken. "This is the Passing Place."

His lips trembled and his eyes watered over. "It is, *Mija*. When we arrived, we didn't know. I have only just figured it out."

My legs gave out on me and I slumped to the ground. Dad knelt with me and we held each other tightly.

CHAPTER 20

I didn't know how long I was in my dad's arms, but it wasn't nearly long enough. I wanted to stay with him, find Mom, and forget all my worries. But I still didn't know where she was.

Doing my best to steady my breathing and hold myself together, I pulled back. "Dad, where's Mom?"

He glanced beyond me. "She is on the other side of the meadow. I can take you over there, but there's something you need to know first. Something I haven't been able to confirm yet."

Looking down at my legs, I saw they were whisking away. *Not yet!*

"Dad!" I hollered, reaching for him—but my hand met only cold air. A shock of icy pain tore through me as the world gave way beneath my feet. I fell, tumbling through darkness, the sound of my own heartbeat echoing in my ears until, with a violent jolt, I slammed back into myself and gasped for air.

For a moment, I didn't know where I was. My chest heaved, lungs burning, heart pounding against my ribs. The scent of lavender was gone. The silence of the Passing Place was gone.

When my vision steadied, I wasn't at the field anymore. I was lying on the couch in the living room. Leaf sat in a chair beside me, elbows on his knees, hands clasped tight, his expression carved with worry —and something heavier.

That's when it hit me all over again. My parents weren't coming back. I had seen them where only the dead belonged.

"Are you all right?"

I was physically fine—but mentally and emotionally destroyed. And I didn't want to talk about it. Least of all with him.

"No," I said, my voice barely above a whisper. I pushed myself upright, every movement slow, like I was trapped underwater. My gaze wandered across the room. The couch. The pictures. The door they'd never walk through again. Like the world had kept going, unaware mine had stopped, the truth pressing so hard against my chest I thought it might break me.

"I need to be alone."

Peeling myself off the couch, I walked in a daze upstairs to my room, not caring if Leaf was behind me or what he was thinking. I *couldn't* care.

When I got to my room, I closed the door and stood perfectly still, not knowing what to do. Cry in bed? Scream at the top of my lungs? Throw my trophies out the window? And what about *Abuela* and Uncle Manny? I could tell Uncle Manny about my parents, but I couldn't tell my *abuela*. She'd just had a heart attack. News of my mom's and dad's death would probably make her have another one. I could't lose her too.

I paced my floor, my breathing shaky and shallow, my tears flowing, and as much as I didn't want to talk to Leaf, I needed *someone.*

With a sharp jerk, I flung my door open. I expected to find him leaning against the wall, aloof or brooding —but instead he was right there at the threshold, eyes wide with concern, chest rising and falling as if he'd been holding his breath.

"Gabriela, what is happening?"

I stepped into his arms and buried my face in his tunic, letting myself feel every shred of emotion swirling inside of me—shock, grief, anger. He held me and stroked my hair, staying with me like that for what seemed like forever while I cried into him.

"What happened, little princess?" he finally asked. "What did you see in your mind?"

I released his hold and took his hand, pulling him over to my bed. We sat on the edge of the mattress, angling our bodies towards each other, our knees touching. He stayed silent, waiting for me to speak. And when I had a handle on my tears, I told him.

"My parents," I whispered, "are dead."

He sucked in his breath, his eyes going from wide to narrow while his hands trembled. He rose to his feet and backed away from me, curling his hands into fists, looking ready to murder someone.

"Draven," he hissed. "Draven did this. I am going to end him one way or another!"

All I could do was nod, letting him know that I wanted Draven gone. More than anything in the world. But there was more I needed to tell Leaf.

"There's more. Something I've known for a while but kept to myself." I steadied my breathing as best as I could. "My dad confirmed that there's a traitor in Strong Haven. He found out from Draven, but he doesn't know who it is. He told me not to trust anyone."

Leaf went still as if I'd knocked the wind out of him. His eyes darkened. "A traitor? For certain?" he repeated, low and sharp.

I nodded, still hardly believing it could be true. "Yes."

Finally confiding in him felt freeing, because now I had someone who could help me figure everything out. Though it didn't remove any of the pain of losing my parents, killing Draven would. And for that to happen, we needed that aquoise.

Aquoise was now the answer for everything.

Lost in my thoughts of grief and revenge, I didn't notice Leaf coming back to me until he knelt on the floor, wrapped his arms around my waist, and placed his head on my lap. "I am so sorry you have lost your parents. So very sorry. I only wish I could have been there to stop it."

His feeling touched my heart, and the love I had for him grew inside of me. I placed my hands under his chin and lifted his face, taking in the raw emotion in his extraordinary eyes.

"I am wretched, Gabriela." His voice broke like

something inside him had cracked open. "I pulled away from you because I do not deserve you. I have done terrible things. Things I cannot take back, or even make right. I am broken, and I do not know how to be with someone the way I want to be with you. Not at all. I do not want to hurt you, but I know I will."

The air between us pulsed with his confession. His words lodged in my chest, sharp and unrelenting. Part of me wanted to draw back, but the greater part wanted to reach for him—to take that anguish and make it mine. He looked shattered, and yet I couldn't stop seeing the pieces of light still left in him.

"I don't care what you've done," I said, voice trembling. "I only care about who you are when you're with me."

He drew a breath that sounded like surrender, his gaze locking on mine with aching intensity. "Then let me lose myself in you."

The space between our lips disappeared as our bodies connected in the deepest, most tender way while we soothed the pain inside of each other with our intimacy.

There was an urgency without rushing, a yearning combined with the deepest understanding. We needed this. We needed each other. And amidst our pulsing passion, we promised that no matter what, we would fight to be together at the end of this.

Staring at the ceiling with Leaf beside me, I forced my sorrow away, telling myself I'd mourn later when this was all over; otherwise, I'd never get through this. And so I started formulating a plan. Our mission was to find the aquoise. If it wasn't in my house or at the bakery, then I had no other choice than to try and communicate with my dad again, because clearly he and my mom had stored the stone somewhere else. Plus, I really needed to see my mom.

"What are you thinking?" Leaf asked, his fingertips trailing up and down my body.

Sunlight flooded through my window blinds, the idea of a bright day prodding me into action. "'I'm thinking we need to find the aquoise."

He lifted my hand to his mouth and kissed my palm. "I am thinking the same. But before we do, I want to remind you that you are now the head of Strong Haven and the High Queen of Faevenly. Once you are crowned, that is."

I gulped. "Oh my gosh, you're right."

I had been so consumed by my parents' death, and then lost in my connection with Leaf, that I hadn't thought about my new role. I sat up, pressing my fingers to my mouth, trying to understand what that really meant for me.

Leaf propped himself up on his arm. "It is not something to cause you alarm. Or anything you need to focus on. But it is who you are now."

His words eased me some. "You're right. I don't

need to focus on that. But we do need to focus on the aquoise."

"Agreed."

We got up and dressed quickly, then once again went back to the kitchen so I could try to contact my dad. But before we sat down, the doorbell rang.

My brows stitched as I looked in the direction of the front door, then back at Leaf. "I wonder who that is?"

Uncle Manny had a key, so he would've let himself in. And it was still early in the morning. Other than the occasional neighbor, we didn't get many visitors. Suddenly, I had an idea of who it was.

"I bet it's my cousin," I said, feeling terrible that I hadn't checked my phone since I'd been back from Faevenly. And knowing Aliana, she'd been trying to reach me.

"It is not safe," Leaf warned.

"I know. But I need to see if it's her, and if so, let her know I'm okay. Then I can ask her to leave. Wait here."

I hurried to the door, When I got there, I peered out the peephole, and I was right. It was Aliana. I opened the door and her big brown eyes enlarged behind her black-rimmed glasses.

"*Prima*! What the hell?" She stepped into the house and gave me a quick, hard hug, then rattled on before I could say anything. "Why didn't you tell me you were back? I've been so worried, and I've been texting!" And then she waved her hands in the air. "Actually, forget that right now. I saw on the news this morning that someone broke into the bakery last night! Like, blew out the back door! What happened?"

I scratched my head, shuffling through everything quickly and deciding to tell her the bare minimum. "I know, I'm sorry. But everything's been happening so fast."

She pushed her glasses up her nose. "Like what?" she asked. "What's been happening? I mean, *Abuela* said you went to Faevenly, but she didn't say why." She stepped closer to me and examined my face. "Your skin looks amazing, by the way. Are you using a new moisturizer or something? You're, like, glowing."

A slight flush warmed my cheeks as my thoughts drifted to Leaf. "No, I'm not wearing anything new."

"Oh, okay. Well, what's been happening?" She folded her arms and tilted her head, waiting for my explanation.

"There's a bunch of stuff going on in Faevenly. *Abuela*, Uncle Manny, a fae guy named Leaf, and I were at the bakery looking for something that we needed. While we were there, some crazy fae witch broke in and *Abuela* had a heart attack."

She slammed her hands across her mouth. "*Ay, Dios mío*. Is she okay?"

"She is. Uncle Manny is with her at the hospital. She had a stent put in and she's expected to come home tomorrow. I'm sure Uncle Manny will tell everyone when he has the chance."

"And your parents? Were they there?" she asked.

A surge of sorrow filled me as I thought of them,

but I didn't have time to get into all that. "No, they're in Faevenly right now."

She kept her hand on her heart for a while. "Thank goodness *Abuela* is okay, and all of y'all. And that your parents weren't there. I'll have to tell my mom and dad right away."

She shifted her cross-body purse in front of her and fished out her phone and started clicking away.

"Um," I said. "This really isn't a good time for me. And don't you have to go to school?"

She kept her head tilted down at her phone but raised her eyes at me. "I can be late. Are you coming to school? You've missed so much already."

Uncle Leto had said school was useless. Now I knew the hard truth of that. At least for me, anyway. I had never fit in at school, not ever. Even when I had tried so hard. Now, I was a future fae queen. My heart and soul belonged in Faevenly. Not in the human realm. I knew that now.

But I couldn't say that to Aliana.

"I'm not going to school today. I need to wait for Uncle Manny and *Abuela*. There's also that thing I need to find. It's really important to Faevenly."

She slipped her phone back in her purse. "What is it?" she asked, with wide eyes. "A sword or a potion or a magic crystal ball?"

"No, but I guess it's close. It's a stone."

Her eyes dazzled. "Whoa, a stone? Like the sorcerer's stone? Like full-on Harry Potter?"

A honk sounded from her car out in front, and I looked over her shoulder. "Is someone with you?"

She rolled her eyes. "It's Carlos. He needed a ride." She turned and waved to him then brought her attention back to me. "Um, I want to hear more about this, but I gotta go. " She grabbed my hand and squeezed. "Please, respond to my text messages so I don't freak out. Okay?"

"I will."

She started to dash off but quickly turned around and came back. "Hey, about that stone you're looking for. You should try the woods behind your house. Remember how when we were little, we'd go in there at night and we thought we could see sparkly things? And your mom and dad would yell at us and tell us not to go in? I bet there's fae stuff back there." She pinned me with a look, then said, "Let me know if you find it."

Closing the door, I thought of the woods and how we were so scared to go in there. I saw my first *muerto* there. That's also where my mom and dad would go whenever they used the shimmer to visit Faevenly." A surge of hope bubbled within me. Aliana was right; it had to be filled with fae stuff.

"We should check it out," Leaf said from behind me.

I spun around, my chest thumping. "You can't sneak up on me like that!"

He smiled. "I was not sneaking." He crossed his arms while a serious look moved across his face. "But if the woods do indeed sparkle, and if Celyse and Julio spent time out there, then the aquoise could indeed be hidden in the trees."

"I agree, and it makes perfect sense." I took one of the fighting sticks that we kept by the front door. "Let's go look."

He laced his fingers through mine and led me to his gear in the kitchen. He took his bow and quiver and slung it over his shoulder, reaching back and pulling his long dark hair out of the way. He was already wearing a belt around his waist for his dagger, but he drew it out to inspect it before placing it back.

Watching him sent my stomach fluttering and my heart soaring. But as I admired his perfect face, a somber shadow crept across. As if a horrible thought had invaded his mind.

"What is it?" I asked.

He strode over to me and took my hands. "If we find the aquoise, we will be set on a course neither one of us can control. And I want you to remember, really remember, what we shared here."

I lifted myself on my toes and kissed him. "I know things will be insane when we return to Faevenly, but I also believe we have a lot of power when it comes to what we want to do."

He looked down for a few seconds. "Sometimes even the most powerful can be rendered powerless."

I blinked, not liking his pessimism at all, but also understanding it. So far, nothing had been going our way but I had to believe all that was about to change.

"Come, little queen," he said, pulling my hand. "Let us do what we came here to do."

A cool breeze swept over my lakeside home, the kind that sifted through your hair with a soft touch and separated each strand piece by piece. It was perfect weather for sitting outside with a blanket and reading, listening to the rustling of leaves and the melody of windchimes. Or perfect for searching for a mysterious blue stone.

"Do you think the wards include the woods?" I asked Leaf in a hushed voice as we stood on the back patio surveying the tall dense trees. "Having Draven swoop in and obliterate us to bits right now would really mess up our mission of finding the aquoise."

"I am confident the wards include the woods. They are part of your home, much like the gardens of Strong Haven or any other palace. And yes, Draven appearing now would complicate things. But I do not think we should worry about that."

We walked away from the house, our boots crunching over grass and leaves, then slipped through the tall oak and cedar trees. The further we moved in, the darker it got, until it almost seemed to turn from day to night.

I slowed my stride and peered up at the sky. Only soft gray blue light could be seen, like the kind you see at dusk that made everything dimly visible. "I swear it just got dark."

Leaf followed my line of sight, then swept his gaze

all around before bringing it back down on me. "These are fae woods."

I gulped, slowing my pace to look around. "These are what?"

"You are more human than fae, and I am more fae than human. So fae things are hard for you to spot. But this is like a piece of Faevenly. Let me show you."

He lifted his face and closed his eyes, breathing in deep. "Smell that?"

I did the same and closed my eyes, taking a long inhale of the air. "I smell trees, dirt, grass and…" Other scents began filtering through my nose. Faint at first, and then stronger. They were sweet and spicy and filled with familiarity. Trying to distinguish them I said, "Clove and vanilla and fresh oranges."

I gazed up at him and he nodded. "Very good."

He continued walking, approaching various tree trunks, placing his hands on them as he walked by. I copied his motions. "What are you feeling for?"

"We will know it when we come upon it," he answered in an almost reverent tone.

Our patch of woods seemed endless as we continued on, touching the rough bark of the trees, checking thick prickly bushes, and poking around rocks and brush. When I thought we'd never find anything, a hard wind erupted from the earth and blasted around us, circling our bodies like a demonic whirlwind.

"I think we found it!" I hollered.

Leaf jerked me to him and I buried my face in his

chest, protecting myself from the onslaught of sticks and dirt that pummeled my back and scraped my exposed skin. I was struggling to nudge even closer when something snatched me by the waist and wrenched me away. Peeking down I saw a thick and knotty branch wrapped around me, tightening like a snake. I pounded at it with my fists as it dragged me to a nearby trunk. Crisscrossing tendrils of bark crossed my body until I was rendered immobile.

"Leaf!" I screamed. The wind around him sped up until I couldn't see him anymore. Turning my attention to what held me, I yelled, "Let me go!"

"We are protecting you, young princess," a smooth but low voice vibrated in my ear. "He is almost gone."

The trees wanted to kill Leaf? "No!" I cried. "He is with me!" And then I remembered who I was. "I command you to release him!"

The wind died down in an instant. The leaves and sticks fell to the ground revealing Leaf alive and crouched on the ground. He dashed over to me as the limb released my body and I scurried away from the tree.

"What in the hell was that?" I asked Leaf, catching my breath.

"A dryad," he answered, examining the nearby trees. "An angry one."

I gaped at him. "A what?"

"A dryad is a spirit that lives in the trees," he explained. "They protect the woods. They must have been brought here by Julio and Celyse. Or Lord Letormis. She is here, but I do not know where."

Walking in a small circle, I examined the trees. "Come out," I said. "We don't mean any harm."

A towering, slender body of moss and leaves stepped out of the trunk. She had sharply pointed facial features and sparkling yellow eyes. She raised her arms out to her sides and bowed low.

"I am Genova, keeper of these trees." She righted herself, then said, "I knew you when you were young, Princess Gabriela. But I see that you do not remember me. It is no matter." She searched about with her glowy eyes. "Where is Princess Celyse?"

A lump formed in my throat and I swallowed it away. "My mother and my father are in the Passing Place."

She hopped back, her branchy brows stitching together and her mossy lips turning downward. "Your mother and father are no more?"

"That's right," I said. "They are no more."

She swooped in close to me and placed her head on top of mine, wrapping her arms around me as leaves fell down from her and circled our feet like a wreath. "I am filled with great sorrow, young one, and my heart is heavy. Princess Celyse spent much time here. Her spirit was pure."

"Thank you, Genova," I said, wrapping my arms around her in return. She smelled of leaves and herbs and reminded me of the cabinet in my house where

Mom kept her teas and herbal remedies. "She did love it out here."

Her hold around me tightened, and she pulled me away from Leaf. "But this one," she hissed, pointing at him, "is not pure."

Twigs and branches from the trees around us shot out, aiming straight for Leaf but staying suspended in the air without touching him. He remained still, keeping his cool. "You are correct. I am not pure, and I have already confessed it to future High Queen Gabriela. I can assure you I do not mean the trees any harm. I am only here to help Gabriela find the aquoise stone. Strong Haven has been targeted by all the other provinces save one, and it is vulnerable."

Genova swung her head toward me. The gleam from her yellow eyes lit up her face, showcasing the different shades of green in the leaves and moss that made up her skin. "Is this true? Is Strong Haven vulnerable?"

"Yes, and we really need the aquoise."

She released her hold and strode around me in a circle, her movements steady and graceful, her mossy steps padding softly against the grass and leaves. "I will show the young princess and future High Queen where the aquoise is. But the impure one must remain where he is."

Leaf nodded. "I am fine with that arrangement."

I didn't like the idea of leaving Leaf, or him being referred to as impure, but I knew I could trust Genova. After all, she was only doing what she thought was in my best interest. And if Genova was a friend to my mother, then she was a friend to me too.

"I'll be right back," I said to Leaf.

Genova waved me to follow her, and we headed further into the woods. After a few minutes, we came upon a cluster of trees and bushes.

"I didn't think these woods were so deep," I marveled.

"These woods appear small on the outside, but once you are inside, they are quite vast. As the daughter of Princess Celyse and steward of this property, you should know that there are many hideaway places. Like this one. Many were put here before, by Trealiorn, others put here in the now, by Celyse."

She gestured to a cluster of thick bushes with a wave, and the vines and leaves rustled apart like a jungle curtain opening.

"Whoa," I said in a half-whisper. "What is this?"

"You may enter and see for yourself," Genova said.

In complete awe of the woodsy hideout, I approached the opening and stepped through carefully. Genova followed. Once we were inside, the foliage closed and a floating orb of light illuminated, like the kind that lined the pathways of the gardens at Strong Haven, revealing a large open space filled with wooden boxes. She went to a smaller one and plucked it from its spot.

She extended it to me. "Here it is. The last remaining piece of aquoise."

I took the box and opened it. Nestled inside on a

bed of leaves was the stone I had seen in the picture, the one I had worn on my necklace. Relief soared through me and a smile spread across my face. Now we had a chance against the other provinces.

"Thank you so much, Genova." I closed the box and held it tight. "This will save Strong Haven."

She smiled wide, showcasing her wood-nubbed teeth, then spun in a circle. The twigs and leaves that formed her long hair lifted with her motion. When she finished, she brought her face close to mine again.

"I am most pleased to have aided you, young princess and future High Queen."

With the box in hand, I followed Genova back to Leaf. My heart elevated with excitement, my fingers trembling as I clutched the box tight. I'd actually done it. *We'd* done it. For the first time, hope didn't feel so far away.

As I stepped toward Leaf, Genova and the branches that had been aimed like weapons slowly receded, curling back into the earth and trees until the forest looked untouched, as if it had all been a dream.

Leaf came forward, his eyes flicking from the retreating vines to the box in my hands. He moved with the caution, as if approaching an ancient weapon. "The aquoise is in there?"

"Yes." My voice shook with relief. I lifted the lid and showed him the shimmering stone resting inside, glowing faintly like captured moonlight. My chest swelled with hope, fierce and bright. "Now we can save Strong Haven."

CHAPTER 21

The woods changed with each step closer to my house. The tall trees and wild brush that had been growing close together began spreading out, making room for human civilization. The darkness overhead that blanketed the acreage began to lighten, as if the sunshine had been given permission to send down its golden rays.

With the aquoise in hand, the transformation signaled hope, and for the first time I thought things might be going our way.

But when I looked at Leaf, I saw a different kind of change.

Instead of being relieved we'd found the stone, he seemed withdrawn and tense. His jaw clenched, his shoulders were tight, his hands curled into fists at his sides. It was as if he was so weighed down by the impending conflict that awaited us in Faevenly, he couldn't see the advantage we now had. Not that I could blame him. He'd been through a lot. And so I let him keep his silence as we trudged along.

By the time we stepped inside the house, he was so

detached he couldn't look at me. It was beginning to scare me.

I tilted my head, trying to read his thoughts. "Leaf, what is it?"

He took the box out of my hands and set it on the kitchen counter. "I told you, everything is going to change now."

With my brows stitched together, I went up to him and cupped his face with my hands. "It might. But we have a chance now, a real chance. And we said we would fight to be together at the end of all this. Remember?"

"Will we? Will you?" He walked away from me, his hands opening and closing at his sides. "I have done horrible things. Things I cannot undo. Things that are not me." He gulped. "The dryad saw right through me. I am impure. You will see too."

My mind spun because I thought we were past all this. "Forget the dryad. You told me this already, you confessed your wrongdoings. All of that is behind us. We just need to get the aquoise back to Strong Haven and fight like hell against the other provinces. After we win and rebuild, then we can be together. Forever."

"And what of Draven? And his traitor?" he asked, continuing to pace the room. "What of them?"

My heart hurt at the anguish surging out of him. Watching him in pain was almost unbearable, and I wanted more than anything to make it go away.

I took his hands and held them to my heart. "We'll figure it out. I promise. I am not giving up on Faevenly or Strong Haven, and I'm certainly not giving up on you. You mean too much to me."

He released my grip, looking wild and on edge, ready to explode. "The thing is, I have already figured it out," he uttered, looking devastated.

I pulled in my chin. "What are you talking about?"

"The traitor."

My heart skipped a beat. "You figured out who the traitor is?"

He walked over and stood in front of me, studying my eyes before he touched my face and kissed me, pouring love into each brush of our lips. With my head in the clouds, I started to slip my arms around him to pull him closer, but he stopped me with a firm grip of my shoulders. He placed me at arms length. He took two steps back.

"Gabriela. I am the traitor."

I stared at him, stunned, the words not landing at first—like they were bouncing off the edges of my mind, refusing to take shape. I shook my head, slow at first, then harder, as if I could physically shake the meaning away. As if I wasn't hearing things right. "What?"

He didn't answer right away, and that silence was worse than any denial. "*I* am the traitor," he said again, this time more forcefully.

My pulse roared in my ears. The walls around us seemed to blur, fading into nothing, his voice and the unbearable truth hanging between us.

"No," I whispered. "That's not possible. You... you *can't* be."

"It is possible, and it is true."

My breath hitched. My blood chilled. I couldn't move as my brain struggled with his words. I stumbled back, clutching my shirt, my heart shattering into a million pieces.

My mind wrestled with what he was telling me, my heart refusing to believe it. I scrambled for ways to prove him wrong. "B-b-but you were with me in the human realm when Draven escaped. In this very house. You've saved me multiple times, beginning with the parking lot. "

"Saving you is one thing, betraying you is another," he said. "As for Draven's escape, he timed his exit when I was here so that none would suspect me."

"No, no, no," I muttered. "Please, stop."

He kept his intense gaze on me. "Back in Strong Haven, when you wanted to know about the creatures of Faevenly, I failed to tell you about the deadliest one of all. Fae. We are cunning and devious and calculating. Able to hide truths and spin the deadliest tales. Now I am taking this aquoise for Draven, even though my doing so is hurting the only one I have ever loved. Do you understand?"

"This can't be happening," I muttered.

"It can, and it is." His hands shook, and his face looked pained as he opened the box, took out the stone, and placed it in his pocket. "I beg you not to follow me."

He spun on his heels and walked toward the front door. I stood there dumbfounded, still putting the pieces together, when the horrible meaning behind his words crashed down on me.

He was acting for Draven. He had released Draven. He was responsible for Draven killing my mom and dad, and Aunt Pen, and all the other fae of Strong Haven. My *abuela* almost died too, except I had somehow saved her life. Now Draven would have the aquoise, the only thing that could save Strong Haven.

Anger boiled up inside me. My parents died because of Leaf. No way in hell was I going to let him leave with that stone.

I raced to the door as he stepped out, grabbing the fighting stick by the stairs. I raised it for a strike, but Leaf spun around, whipped out his own stick in a flash, and parried my blow with ease.

"Gabriela, do not do this."

I jabbed, Leaf deflected. I raised my stick, ready to strike again. "You killed my parents," I spat, wanting nothing more than to take him down so I could get that stone.

He lowered his weapon to the ground and raised his hands. "Please, stop this. I do not want to hurt you."

"You killed my parents!"

I lunged, but Leaf sidestepped my strike. He swooped in and grabbed me by the throat. His sparkling blue eyes darkened, his face painted with dominance. Panic rushed over me like an icy blast as my body went numb.

I had no idea what he was doing to me.

"**Hear me.**" The low octave of his voice froze me in place while my body went slack and my stick tumbled out of my grasp. My will was no longer mine, but his. Nothing else mattered or existed but what he wanted.

"**Stop fighting me.**"

He released me but stayed close, and I watched as the blue color returned to his eyes. He moved in and whispered against my ear, "I am sorry. For everything. I pray you can understand and forgive me one day."

As if stuck in a waking nightmare, I remained still —unable to blink, barely able to breathe—while he walked away. I didn't know how long I stayed like that before I regained my senses and control of my body and remembered who I was and what I was doing.

I was attacking Leaf, the traitor. He took my aquoise and spelled me so I'd stop fighting him.

I raced down the front walkway and into the street, whipping my gaze about, unable to see where he had gone. Not even believing that the one I had fallen in love with had betrayed me.

CHAPTER 22

I went back inside my house, lowered myself onto the kitchen floor, and sat there stunned and hollowed. Shivers flowed across my body and a permanent knot gouged my gut. I had lost everything and didn't know how much more pain and suffering I could endure. It was taking every ounce of sheer will to not fall apart completely.

But I wasn't alone for long. The front door swung open and footsteps sounded as someone headed toward the kitchen.

"Gabriela? Leaf? It's Manny. Uncle Manny."

I could see the top of his head as he stalled by the kitchen table, but I knew he couldn't see me over the counter.

"I'm down here," I said in a small voice.

He came around to the sink and found me on the floor. He looked down at me and must have seen my pain, my heartbreak, and my numbness. He joined me right away.

"*Mija*, what's going on? Why are you down here?" He looked around. "Where's Leaf?"

There was so much I needed to tell him, but I had

to pull myself together first. I could feel my tears creeping up, threatening to gush out. I forced myself to harden so they wouldn't take over. There was no time for that. Not now anyway.

"It's awful, Uncle Manny," I whispered. "So awful."

He scooted in with tender eyes and rubbed my knee. "What's awful?"

The truth was awful. Leaf being a traitor and leaving wasn't even the worst of it, but it was the freshest blow. I leaned into my uncle and stayed like that for a while, mustering the strength to tell him the hardest news.

"It's Mom and Dad." I wiped the lone tear that trailed down my cheek and swallowed hard. "They're dead."

His body stiffened, as if he'd been jolted. "They're... dead?"

"Yes," I nodded. "My dad connected with my mind and took me to the Passing Place, where fae go in Faevenly when they die. He said Mom is there too, and they ended up there after Draven attacked them. I wanted to tell you but hadn't had the chance yet, what with everything that happened at the bakery and *Abuela's* heart attack."

He sat still for a few long seconds. "Are you sure?" he asked, needing confirmation. "Maybe your dad got it wrong. Maybe he was confused."

I wiped the tears from my eyes. "I'm sure. I saw it myself."

He wrapped me in his arms and held me tight as

soft weeping sounds came from him. "*Dios mío*," he muttered. "Not your mom and dad. Not after everything."

I went totally numb after Uncle Manny said that, but I continued to stay there pressed up against him, finding comfort in his embrace as my own tears flowed.

He reached up and snatched a dish rag from the counter. He handed it to me so I could wipe my eyes, then used his sleeve to wipe his.

"Where is Leaf?" he finally asked, his voice crackled and breaking. "Is he okay?"

I had been waiting for him to ask, and dreaded telling him. Uncle Manny already had strong feelings about Leaf. And despite what he had done, I still didn't understand how he could've turned traitor.

"Leaf is gone."

"Gone? What do you mean?"

"We found the aquoise. Out in the wooded area behind the house," I said quietly.

"Thank goodness," he exhaled. "That's great news."

I wrapped my arms around my stomach. "Not really, because Leaf took it. I tried to fight him and get it back, but he did some sort of magic on me. Then he left."

"Magic? What do you mean?" He sat back with a scowl on his face. "Why did he take it?"

"Because, Uncle Manny... he's the traitor. That's why."

Confusion covered Uncle Manny's tired and worn

face. "He is what?" He moved away from me so we were facing each other. "What did you say?"

"He told me he's the traitor. Then he took the aquoise and said he was taking it to Draven. I tried to stop him but couldn't, and then he left."

Uncle Manny ran his hands through his hair and pulled. "If he is working with Draven, then he is the one who set Draven free. Without Leaf's help, Draven wouldn't have been able to get near your parents. Faevenly wouldn't be in this level of danger."

"I know," I whispered.

"He killed your parents," he uttered.

Leaf was responsible for my parents' death, there was no doubt. Though somehow, deep down inside, I found myself struggling with that truth because it didn't make sense.

Fury crept into Uncle Manny's eyes as he rose to his feet and stomped over to the back door. I stood and watched as he jerked it open, went outside, and hollered at the top of his lungs. Then he grabbed the cushions off the outdoor furniture and started chucking them across the yard one by one, grunting and panting.

"I knew it! I knew he couldn't be trusted!"

I stayed by the door, watching his explosion, understanding his display. If I hadn't felt so crushed and empty, I would've thrown stuff too.

When everything on our patio had been hurled onto the lawn, he slumped to the stone pavement. I approached him with caution and joined him.

"What do we do now?" I asked.

He covered his face with his hands. "I don't know. I-I-I need a minute."

I pulled my knees up to my chest and wrapped my arms around my legs, waiting for Uncle Manny to come up with something. Anything. My brain wasn't working, and if I started strategizing, I'd start thinking about everything that had happened. I wasn't ready for that yet.

"Okay," Uncle Manny finally said. "I know what to do. We go to Faevenly and tell Leto everything. Then we find Draven and Leaf and kill them and get that stone."

Kill Leaf?

Uncle Manny rose to his feet, and I followed, my mind spinning at his plan. We definitely needed to find Draven and end him once and for all. But Leaf?

Trudging back inside, I replayed Leaf's confession in my mind. He was in pain. He didn't want to hurt me. His hands were shaking. But one statement overrode all the others. Before he had taken the aquoise, he talked about fae being able to hide truths and spin the deadliest tales. Then he asked me if I understood. I steadied my hands on our quartz counter, trying to figure out what he meant by that.

What did he want me to understand?

I thought of asking Uncle Manny but didn't think it was a good idea. He had already tried and convicted Leaf in his mind the second Leaf stepped into my life.

I'd have to ask Uncle Leto. Or Lady Sonia. They might know what Leaf meant.

"Gabriela, are you okay?"

"Yes—I mean, no. I mean…"

"I know, I feel the same. But we need to focus."

I swallowed. "Okay, yeah, focus."

"Do you have a shimmer?" Uncle Manny asked.

"I do. The one Lady Sonia gave me when Leaf and I came for the aquoise."

"Good, we're going to need it," he said. He brought out his phone and started texting, As he clicked away, he explained, "I'm texting the other *tios y tias*, telling them we're going to Faevenly right away. One of them can take care of *Abuela*."

"Are you going to tell them about my mom and dad?"

"No," he answered quickly. "Not with *Abuela* still in recovery. We can tell everyone later, when this whole thing is over."

I nodded in response, thinking it would never be over, then asked, "What about the bakeries? And school?"

"I'm already on it," he said. "I'm texting *Tia* Maria so she can handle telling the school. I'm also alerting the bakery managers of my absence."

Impressed with Uncle Manny's focus and speed, a side of him I didn't see very often, I thought I should text Aliana.

"I'll be right back," I muttered.

He lowered his phone. "Where are you going?"

Pointing upstairs, I said, "To my room to get a few things."

He hesitated then nodded. "Hurry."

I left Uncle Manny and went upstairs, then lowered myself onto the edge of my bed. I ran my hands over my crumpled sheets, feeling the soft cotton against my skin, thinking how not long ago I'd been in Leaf's arms. Now he was the enemy, right next to Draven.

I couldn't believe it.

I studied my room, taking everything in—my books, my pictures, my trophies. All the things that made me human. All the things that didn't really fit me. At least not anymore, now that I was caught up in the perils of the fae realm.

Dreading texting my cousin, I forced myself to get my phone I had left on my desk. With a touch, it sprang to life, and I was surprised it still had any battery left. I texted Aliana.

Hey, *prima*. We found the stone. It was like you thought, hidden in the woods. But now it's been...

My fingers hovered over the phone, trying to figure out what to say.

... stolen. And taken to Faevenly. Uncle Manny and I are going to get it. We'll be fine. Back in a few days

Three blinking bubbles popped up right away letting me know she was texting back, but I didn't have it in me to answer any questions. So I turned my phone off and set it back on my desk, not caring to plug it in, because I knew I'd be gone for a long while.

"Gabriela, you ready to go?" Uncle Manny shouted from downstairs.

"Yeah, just a sec." I smoothed back my hair and checked myself in the mirror. My brown eyes were bloodshot, the skin around them puffy.

I considered putting on makeup, but it wouldn't help. I was too far gone for that. Packing a bag crossed my mind too—but for what? Nothing here would help me over there.

I still had my hoop earrings and my cross. That was all I needed. That, and the shimmer Lady Sonia had given me. I had slipped it into my jeans pocket when I changed out of my dress. I reached in with my fingers. It was still there.

Turning off my light, I gave everything one last look, then shut the door. I hurried downstairs and joined Uncle Manny in the kitchen.

He clapped his hands together. "All right, I've turned off all the lights and locked the doors. Are you ready to do this?"

I studied my uncle, thinking how relieved I was to have him going back to Faevenly with me. He knew the fae. He knew the realm. He'd know how to handle things.

I gave him a hug, then said, "I'm glad you'll be with me."

He hugged harder, "Me too, *Mija*."

Taking the shimmer out of my pocket, I extended it until it stretched out tall enough and wide enough for Uncle Manny and me to step through with ease. With the Strong Haven garden coming into view, Uncle Manny motioned for me to go first. With a whoosh, I hopped over, and he followed. I quickly collapsed the portal until it was small enough to return to my pocket.

Now to find Uncle Leto and tell him what had happened.

And figure out what to do next.

CHAPTER 23

C hatter filled the air, along with the pounding of boots and clanking of weapons. A group of five guards raced by us, then another two in the opposite direction.

"Oh no," Uncle Manny muttered. "The other provinces. They must be almost here."

"Must be," I added. "We need to hurry and find Uncle Leto."

A couple of maid servants scurried by, and I lunged for the shoulder of one. She was small and petite like the ones who were always with Maid Gidna, but this one had short silver hair, not brown hair.

"Excuse me, where is Leto, I mean, Lord Letormis?"

"Princess Gabriela," she said with a low bow. "He is in the war room with his advisors."

"War room?" I asked. I hadn't heard of a room like that in the palace. "Where is that?"

"The opposite corridor from the Great Hall," she answered. "You cannot miss it."

"Thank you," I said before she scurried off.

"The Great Hall," Uncle Manny said with a slight shudder. "I know exactly where that is. Come on."

We hurried inside, passing more guards and maid servants while making our way up and down corridors until we came to a well-guarded set of doors. They were simple and functional, made of thick dark wood, but intimidating all the same.

The guards recognized me right away. With a bow, they quickly pulled on the heavy handles. We walked through a small hallway that opened up to a large room with dark walls, a dark stone floor, and a massive round wooden table. Glowing orbs floated along the ceiling for light. Guards lined the perimeter, and sitting at the table were Uncle Leto, Lady Sonia, Dain, Githion, and Rook. They rose to their feet when we entered.

"Gabriela, and Manny," Uncle Leto said with relief. "Come, sit. We are most relieved to see you. Please tell us your good news."

With a sideways glance to Uncle Manny, followed by a gulp, we approached the table. Uncle Leto motioned us to two open chairs, and we settled in.

"Where is Leaf?" Rook asked with a raised brow.

"Hey, Rook," Uncle Manny said with a nod. "It's good to see you."

"Manny," Rook replied back with a stiff nod.

Uncle Manny tapped his fingers on the table and cleared his throat. "Leaf isn't with us anymore." He glanced my way and asked in a low voice, "Want me to explain, or do you want to?"

"I'll do it," I said.

Rook's brows stitched, as did Leto's, and all eyes

swung to me. Telling them that Leaf took the stone for Draven, and all the implications that flowed from that, was going to be a huge blow. I had to be sure to say the right things.

I cleared my throat like Uncle Manny had and did my best to sit tall while my hands clenched together on my lap. "Leaf and I found the aquoise. The last remaining piece."

"Wonderful news!" Githion exclaimed, slapping his thick hands on the table. "Now we can—"

I cut him off with a raise of my hand and shook my head. "That's not all."

Githion clamped his mouth shut in surprise while Uncle Leto leaned in with narrowed eyes and a serious look. "Go on," he prodded.

Lowering my hands back to my lap, I forced my heartbeat to steady as much as possible before I continued. "Leaf and I found the stone in a place where my parents had hidden it, but then Leaf took it and left."

"Took it?" Uncle Leto pulled his chin in, exchanging glances with Lady Sonia and then Rook. "Explain."

Taking in a deep breath I said, "Leaf took the aquoise so he could give it to Draven, and he confessed to being the traitor and setting Draven free."

Rook exploded from his seat. "No! I do not believe that! Leaf may be reckless and impulsive, and he may defy authority, but he would never align with the likes of Draven Midlothian! Not ever!" Fury filled his eyes, and his breathing came out in ragged, short bursts.

I forced my voice to stay calm yet authoritative, the way my mother spoke, and I met Rook's angry eyes. "Leaf *did* take it. He said it was for Draven. Like you, I would have never thought he could do something so heinous. But he did."

I shifted my hands together on my lap, searching for the right words. "But I've been thinking it through, and thinking of the things he told me when he took it, and even before, and I truly believe he didn't do it willingly." I replayed the conversation in my mind. "His hands were shaking and he was clearly in pain before he picked up the stone. It was almost as if he didn't want to do it."

I stopped before I continued, because this part belonged to me, to my memories, but they needed to know more.

"Leaf and I shared something between us. Something powerful and real. Before he left me, he asked me to understand. He also said he hoped that one day I would forgive him. It was almost like a desperate cry for help. I was stunned, just like all of you here."

I paused, wondering if I should tell them about my parents, but quickly decided to save that for the end. I needed to keep my focus on Leaf and what he had done with the aquoise.

"When I realized he was responsible for so much death, I pushed aside my feelings for him and I went after him and fought him. He could have easily killed me, but he did everything possible to leave me unharmed. And when I wouldn't back down, he used magic to stop me. His eyes went dark and his words vibrated low. In a blink, I was frozen. In another blink, he was gone."

Taking one more calming breath, I said, "I think— no, I know—he was spelled to release Draven from the dungeon, find the aquoise, and bring it to him. I believe that in my heart. I just don't know how."

I looked around the table, giving them a nod to signal I was finished.

"You were compelled," Lady Sonia said to me with sorrow and understanding. "When his eyes darkened and you lost control of yourself, it is called being compelled." She met the eyes of everyone in the room. "And it sounds like Draven somehow compelled Leaf."

"Draven is a monster who should have never been allowed to live!" Rook slammed his fists on the wood, sending a crack splitting down the middle. "We should have ended him when we had the chance!"

We should have," Manny said as Rook lowered himself back to his seat. "But it's too late to second guess our decisions."

"But how could Draven have compelled Leaf?" Dain asked. "Leaf' visited rarely, and only trained dungeon guards and Lady Sonia were ever allowed near Draven."

Leto pinched the bridge of his nose. "Leaf visited here two days before Draven escaped."

A horrible silence fell on the room, as if knocking the air right out of everyone. He'd been here.

"He did?" Lady Sonia asked, dumbfounded. "I did not know."

"He did," Leto replied. "He said he was traveling close by and wanted to pay me a visit. He was not here for more than two hours, but during that time he must have made his way to the dungeon unseen."

"Thunderation," Dain uttered.

"And that monster got to him," Githion seethed.

"Fool," Rook said under his breath. "He could never shake the need to end Draven or the Kanes. Never. Now he is lost to us."

My stomach knotted, because I knew Rook was right. Leaf had been carrying a vendetta against the Kanes and Draven for a long time. All the way back to when my parents were here. Whatever plan Leaf had going into that dungeon must have backfired. I felt sick to my stomach.

Lady Sonia placed her hand on Rook's shoulder. "We shall not give up hope. If Leaf has been compelled, we may be able to reverse it with the right help."

"There's more," I said before I lost my nerve. "I saw my dad."

"Your father is in the human realm?" Lady Sonia asked.

"No, Lady Sonia," I said in a broken voice. "Not there."

Uncle Manny reached over and squeezed my hand. "Go on, *Mija.*"

With that nudge of encouragement, I cleared my throat and said, "He and my mother are in the Passing Place. They ended up there after Draven's attack."

Lady Sonia touched her fingertips to her lips, and her eyes teared over. "Oh, my lady. I am so sorry to hear that."

"No." Uncle Leto leaned forward with his hands pressed together and his gaze filled with grief. "My dearest Gabriela. Are you sure?"

"I am," I muttered.

"I am so sorry, my princess," Leto uttered. "So very sorry."

"Sadness aside, and I do offer my condolences, but that makes you the heir apparent, my lady," Dain said to me. "It also makes Leaf equally responsible with Draven for the deaths of Princess Celyse and Lord Julio, a crime of the highest order, no matter if he was coerced or not. And lastly, without the aquoise and with the forces of the other provinces gathering against us, it appears we need a new war strategy."

Uncle Leto rose to his feet and started circling the table. He took long and steady strides while rubbing his hands together. "Princess Gabriela, Strong Haven is yours. I am at your service, as is everyone here at this table."

Everyone murmured their assent and offered me nods and looks of encouragement. "Thank you," I said, trying to hide my terror. "I most definitely need the service of everyone here." I gave my Uncle Leto a look that I hoped conveyed just how much I was going to need him.

"Of course, my queen. And you will have it." He continued pacing, then said, "And for their crimes, Draven and now Leaf are considered enemies of Strong Haven and will be declared wanted for murder."

Rook clenched his fist and ground his words out through his tight jaw. "Leaf should not be so labeled if he was not acting on his own accord."

"The label will be removed if the coercion is proved. But until such time, we can make no assumptions and must operate based on fact. Leaf confessed his involvement to Princess Gabriela. He took the stone for Draven. That is we know for certain."

"Fine," Rook spat, meeting Uncle Leto's gaze with sheer determination. "Assuming we are not all obliterated by the forces descending on us, I request a formal investigation into his intent."

"And you will have it," Leto agreed. "As for the matter of altering our strategy now that we do not have aquoise"—he placed his hands on the table and leaned over—"I see no other option than to abandon Strong Haven."

My mouth fell open. I was not expecting Leto to say that. But as his words worked their way through me, I realized he was right. We were up against four other provinces, and Draven had the aquoise. We didn't stand a chance against them.

"Queen Gabriela," Leto said. "That is what I advise, but the decision is yours."

A warm flush of nervousness crept up my neck, the tingle I had started feeling when Uncle Leto came to my house for my parents still lingered. Our dangers were never-ending now, and I wondered if anything would ever go back to normal.

"Sadly, I agree. I think we should abandon Strong Haven. Does anyone have any reason why we should stay?" I asked.

Another heavy silence fell over the room. Leto broke it with a firm nod. "It is settled, then. We shall abandon Strong Haven."

"Where will we go?" Uncle Manny asked.

"With me," Rook was quick to offer. "To the Sublands. There is plenty of room for everyone. We can strategize our next steps there."

"Thank you, my friend," Leto said. "I was hoping you would make the offer."

"Yes, thank you very much, Rook," I added.

I had a vague idea where the Sublands was, but no clue how long it would take for us to get there. Wanting to hide my ignorance, I kept quiet, waiting for Leto to issue more directives.

"When do we leave?" Lady Sonia asked.

Leto stayed standing and crossed his arms. "We will leave in waves. First wave will include the queen and all the dignitaries, as well as half our forces. They will leave today. I will stay behind with Dain and Githion and bring in the second wave after departure preparations are made. Two days at the most."

"My men and I will travel with the queen," Rook added.

A strange tightness gripped my chest. *Leaving Strong Haven.* The words sounded impossible. This was supposed to be our home, our fortress—the one place that couldn't fall. Now we were abandoning it like a sinking ship. I looked around the council room, half expecting someone to change their mind, but no one did. The plan was set.

With the order issued, the palace exploded with activity as word of the mass exit traveled down the corridors. Uncle Leto had also restricted everyone to one bag only. For me and Uncle Manny, that wouldn't be a problem since we didn't bring anything. But the maid servants had other ideas. They descended on us, charged with efficiently supplying us with proper travel clothes and weaponry.

A group whisked Uncle Manny away, and Maid Gidna came for me. "My dear, my dear," she said, taking me and holding me to her. "I have heard all the news. I am deeply saddened to hear of the passing of Princess Celyse and Lord Julio. Most saddened, especially after knowing the great odds they overcame to be together."

I hugged her back. "Thank you, Gidna."

Releasing me, she bowed low. "And I am most humbled to serve you, my queen."

"Oh Gidna," I said. "I'm still just Gabriela."

She waved at me. "Nonsense." Then she started pulling me along again.

When we got to my room, we found it empty of maid servants. There was only a bag opened on the bed and clothes already stacked inside. I rummaged through them and found undergarments, dresses, boots, and slippers, along with a small pouch of vials and grooming tools. There was also a pair of pants and a tunic tucked at the very bottom.

Gidna cleared her throat as if to avoid talking about what she had clearly snuck in for my comfort. "The dresses are a mix of formal and informal befitting a queen," she explained. "As for what you have on now" —she waved at my jeans with disapproval—"those will not do."

I knew she was right. If I was to be a queen, then I needed to look like one. Sitting on the edge of the bed, I kicked off my boots, then slipped off my shirt and jeans. Gidna came over and handed me what she called a travel dress, though it looked like a formal gown to me. It was a rich dark brown, with stitchings of leaves and vines along the edges. To complete the look, she handed me a matching pair of tall brown boots, and everything fit perfectly.

But as I eyed the stack of my discarded clothes that Gidna had folded, an intense need to keep anything and everything from home flooded me. And that included my jeans, shirt, and boots. I was with my mom when I bought them.

"My queen, are you all right?" Gidna asked. She held up my clothes. "Is it these?"

"If it's all right, I'd like to pack those."

"Of course," she said. She opened the bag and placed them inside. "Anything else?"

Running my hand over the bedsheets, I thought of my first memory in this room. I was around six or seven, and Mom and Dad had brought me here, letting me know this was my mom's room when she was little, and every time we visited, it would be mine. I remembered being excited and scared all at the same time because everything was so big.

"My dear, would you like some alone time?" Gidna asked, pulling me away from the memory.

"Actually, yes. If you don't mind."

With an understanding smile, she nodded. "I will be back when it is time for you to board the carriage."

When she left, I lay down on my side, my thoughts staying on my parents. The last time I saw my dad, we were in the Passing Place meadow. He was about to tell me something and take me to Mom, but we had lost our connection.

Maybe I could reconnect with him now. He needed to know what was happening. And we needed to finish our conversation.

Closing my eyes, I thought of him and Mom. I visualized Dad's short dark hair, brown eyes, and his chiseled features; and mom's long blond hair with her streak of black and her bright green eyes. I thought of how much my parents loved each other, and how much they loved me. My love for them swirled in my heart, filling me up with so much joy, but also so much sadness.

Dad, connect with me. Please. I need you now more than ever.

A soft whisper floated around my head, becoming louder as I focused on it. It was warm and pleasing, and it filled me with comfort.

"¿*Mija*?"

My eyes flung open and I found myself lying on a bed of grass, in the same lavender meadow where I'd last seen my dad. He was sitting across from me now, wearing a smile.

"*Mija*, I am so glad to see you."

I sat up and lunged over to hug him, holding him with all my might. "Me too," I managed to squeak out between the choking sob clogging my throat.

He held me with the same intensity, keeping me close, rocking me gently until he loosened his hold and pulled back. "What is it, *Mija*? What is happening in Faevenly?" he asked with his brow stitched with worry.

"Oh, Dad. A lot and it's all terrible. All the other provinces are marching down on us so Uncle Leto ordered the evacuation of Strong Haven. We're heading to the Sublands today."

"Oh no," he muttered, rubbing his forehead. "Things are that bad?"

I swallowed, scared to tell him the rest, but knowing I needed to. "Things are worse than bad. Leaf and I went looking for the aquoise, hoping the stone could help us. We found it with the help of the dryad, Genova. And then... Leaf took it."

He narrowed his eyes while he processed my words. "Leaf is the traitor?"

Dad always was one to decipher things quickly. "Yes, he is."

"Damn," he said, plucking a sprig of lavender from the meadow. "Damn, damn, damn."

"But Dad..." I drew in a gulp of air. "I think Draven made Leaf do it. I truly in my heart don't believe he could have ever done something like that. Not ever."

He tilted his head and considered me with a knowing look. "You love him."

My eyes watered over, and I tried to fight the tears, but a few spilled out anyway. "I do."

He wrapped his arms around me and held me to him. "It's okay, *mija*. It's okay. I was like you not so long ago, a boy from the human realm falling for a fae. Ours was a forbidden love, but we managed to overcome seemingly insurmountable odds to be together." He stroked my cheek. "So I understand."

We stayed like that for what seemed like forever, and while I was grateful for his understanding, I really needed my mom. "Dad, where is Mom?"

"I will take you to her, but first, I need to explain what I have learned about the Passing Place, something I started telling you last time you were here, but we lost our connection."

"Okay," I whispered. "What is it?"

He sat back, but kept my hands in his. "When we

see the dead, we know they're dead, right? Sometimes we see bullet holes and gashes and blood. If we don't see visible signs of death, we see haziness and other evidence of spiritual form. Like bodies walking through things. Right?"

"Right," I said, not exactly knowing where he was going.

He paused before he continued, making sure I was following along. "Being an Avila means never forgetting those things. But I forgot everything I knew when I first got here, because I was filled with so much grief. And you, as an Avila, need to not forget those things too. They are special and unique to who we are. They are part of our gifts."

Staring at him, my eyes followed the hard lines of his shoulders, the edges of his jaw. I reached out and touched him, poking his chest. "Oh my gosh, Dad! You're alive!"

"I am, *mija*."

My eyes widened and I threw my arms around his neck and hugged him. "Thank you, God!"

He patted my back for a bit before he released me. "But your mom..." He hesitated, shaking his head. "She is not alive, and she doesn't know it."

My mind zipped to Lady Sonia telling me about souls staying in their bodies because they didn't know they were dead. I didn't exactly understand it then, and I didn't understand it now.

"I don't get it."

"I didn't either, and it took me a while to figure it

out. But I've learned that time runs differently here, and her mind has taken her to a safe place before we knew of the unrest in the provinces. Before we left home for the council meeting. She thinks we are here in Faevenly visiting, and that nothing is wrong. And *mija*," his voice cracked. "I can't bring myself to tell her the truth, because if I do, she will leave me."

"Oh, Dad," I muttered, my hands shaking as my body shivered from the heartache he was enduring. A heartache that worked its way through me too.

"It's okay. It really is. She is happy here, and I am happy with her." He glanced around the meadow. "Do you want to see her now?"

I nodded. "Yes."

We rose to our feet and started making our way across the meadow when another question popped in my mind. "How did y'all end up here? In the Passing Place?"

"When Draven attacked us, your mother and I were on opposite ends of the corridor. He flung his energy blast at her first. When his light dissipated, I couldn't see her. Some of our forces charged in, and while Draven was focused on them, I used your mom's shimmer to look for her, and that's how I ended up here with her spirit."

"Mom has a shimmer—or, had a shimmer?"

"Yes, Lady Sonia helped us make shimmers for each other. We even have one for you."

I blinked, slowing down my pace. "You do?"

"Of course. In case you ever needed us physically, we wanted to be able to get to you."

His explanation mostly made sense, in a witchy Avila way. I was still trying to wrap my head around it all when an area with apple trees, flowering bushes, and a creek came into view. And there in the water stood Mom with her long green dress tied up at her knees. She was holding a stick, peering at the water, looking for a fish to spear.

"Celyse, look who I found," Dad called out cheerfully.

She turned around, her long hair flowing around her. She smiled wide. "My beautiful girl!"

Tossing her stick on the grass, she came over to me and hugged me tight. She had a translucent glow about her, but only if you looked closely. I had no idea how we were able to hug, but was so grateful that we could.

"Mom!" I said, relieved to be with her in any form. "I'm so happy to see you."

Her hug threatened to unleash my tears, but I held them in for her sake and stayed in our embrace, letting her love flow over me.

With a kiss on my cheek, she released me with a smile. "Where have you been? We've been waiting for you."

"I, uh," I glanced at dad for help, not knowing what I should say.

"You remember, Celyse," Dad cut in. "Our girl has been studying for that test."

Her brow creased, as if struggling to recall anything

about me needing to study for a test. Then she shrugged and chuckled. "I always forget when you need to study. But it makes no difference. You are finally here."

Dad bent down and plucked two white daisies from a nearby bush. He threaded one behind Mom's ear, and the other behind mine. "My beautiful girls," he said. Then he took our hands. "Why don't we stroll for a bit?"

Walking in between them, I pushed my sadness to the background of my mind because I wanted to be in this moment with Mom and Dad. Safe between them, as if nothing could ever harm me here. We strolled along the creek, stopped to snack on sweet red apples, and even fished for a bit.

Like Dad said, she acted as if everything were normal. There was no turmoil in Faevenly, no evil witch, no cares whatsoever. And I let her stay in that world, understanding exactly why Dad hadn't told her.

The hours rolled by effortlessly, and I almost started forgetting the horrors I had left behind, when Dad brought me back to reality. He told Mom I needed to get back home to study, and she accepted his exit strategy for me with ease.

After I hugged her tightly, Dad walked me back to the meadow. And we didn't say anything for a while.

"Now that your Avila skills are blossoming, you can use your mind to connect with mine and come here anytime," he said. He glanced over his shoulder toward where we had left Mom. "And when it's time for her to move on from here, I'll come back."

My throat tightened. I understood why he wasn't leaving with me—why he'd stayed so calm, so careful. He couldn't tell her the truth. Couldn't tell her that she was already gone. The weight of it pressed on me, sharp and suffocating. And yet, somehow, I knew he was right. Mom deserved peace, and he was the only one who could give it to her.

Around us, the lavender swayed in the breeze, and I hated it for being so beautiful when everything inside me was breaking. My dad was choosing to stay in this place between worlds, so she wouldn't have to face it alone.

"How long will you be?" I asked, my voice trembling even as I tried to keep it steady. I wanted to sound brave, but the words quivered like the petals around us.

He took my hands and squeezed. "Not long, *mija*."

"Okay," I said, though the word barely made it out. The lump in my throat burned, and for the first time since I'd arrived, I wanted to leave—not because I was ready, but because staying any longer was too painful.

"I know you will. Now go, *mija*. This is your time. And Faevenly needs you. Just remember to trust who you are as an Avila and a Strong. Your gifts are powerful and will never fail you."

He hugged me again and kissed my cheek, then backed away with love in his eyes, his body and the meadow around him slowly fading away.

My eyes fluttered open as a soft knock sounded and my door swung open.

"My dear," Maid Gidna said cautiously, "are you well? It is time to go."

I sat up and wiped my face. "I'm fine and I'm well. Thank you, Gidna."

I rose to my feet and scanned the room, admiring it all. The ornately carved wood bed. The silky drapes that framed the oversized arch-shaped window and were a different color each time I visited. The thick white rug that centered the room, soft as clouds beneath me

I had no idea if I'd ever see this place again, no idea what would become of Strong Haven. But I knew this. My mom was born and raised here. This was her home, and so it was mine too.

And I was going to fight like hell for it.

CHAPTER 24

Leaf

She had invaded me. My mind, my heart, my wretched soul—everything, though I tried desperately to not let her. And as I walked away from her, after compelling her for her own good, I refused to look back. It was better that way.

I had let loose a monster who had killed her parents, making me a monster too. I took from her the last remaining piece of aquoise, the final hope for Strong Haven. I had deceived her in the worst way. I was not worthy of someone like Gabriela Sarah Avila.

Monsters did not deserve love.

Walking away from her home, I spotted a secluded area of trees and moved in close. Examining the trunks and the leaves, I smelled the air. Human realm trees. Finally, I had gained enough distance from Julio's and Celyse's fae woods and its watcher, Genova.

With no one around, I slipped through and continued until I was out of sight from the main road. Finding a spot big enough to expand the shimmer, I fished it out of my pocket. I placed it on my palm.

Some shimmers were connected to places, others to fae. This one was given to me and led straight to the source of nightmares, the father of evil himself, Draven. The deadly soul vamp witch had taken control of me with a compulsion when I had tried to kill him in the dungeon.

Now, he owned me.

Clenching my jaw, I stared at the small portal. If I could destroy it, maybe I could go back to Gabriela, take her, explain everything, and beg her forgiveness. We could hide away forever.

But I could not destroy it. I had tried many times and failed.

Staring at my fingers, I tried again. I willed them to close, straining every muscle in my hand in an effort to clamp down so hard I would obliterate the cursed thing. But my body refused to obey. I grunted, pacing around the trees, and leveled one with a punch as I hollered into the wind.

With my fist pressed against the bark, I stayed there, my breathing short and shallow. My mind filled with the faces of the fae whose deaths I had caused when Draven marched his way out of Strong Haven and flung his energy blasts. I imagined Celyse and Julio in the Passing Place. I could not bring them or any other souls back. But I was determined to take Draven's as retribution.

I did not know how. I did not know when. But as sure as a dagger drew blood, his life was mine.

I expanded the shimmer, stretching it out tall and wide. Not recognizing the grassy landscape, and not spotting Draven either, I stepped through.

Safely on the other side, I scanned the area, taking in the scene. Tall blades of grass covered my boots, and a lake was nearby. I could smell the water and hear the lapping of waves as flopping fish slapped the surface.

I collapsed the shimmer and put it back in my pocket, waiting for Draven to reveal himself. "Where are you, you mad witch?" I muttered.

"Hello, Leaf," his sinister voice spoke from behind me. "I trust you have brought me what I sent you for?"

Step by step I turned around to face Draven. He wore his usual dark attire with his long cloak. His hood was down, and he studied me with his menacing crystal eyes.

"I have," I said through clenched teeth, every word burning like ash in my mouth.

He held out his hand. "Very good. Now, come forth."

His command vibrated in my ears, filling my mind. I slowly walked to him, chin raised, brow furrowed as I leveled him with a death stare, fighting each step but unable to stop myself. I came to a halt a few feet away from him.

"I *will* find a way to break your hold on me, Draven," I spat, jaw clenched.

"There is no such thing," he sneered. "You cannot resist my orders, no matter how hard you try. But if you want to be difficult, then I can too."

He flung out his hand, and a blast of red energy slammed into my chest. Fire ripped through my veins, shredding muscle and bone from the inside out. The world tilted—then vanished—as I was hurled backward. I crashed to the ground, the air ripped from my lungs as I hurtled into a tree with bone-jarring force.

For a heartbeat, I couldn't breathe. Couldn't move. The metallic tang of blood filled my mouth, warm and slick. I spat it out, wiped my lips, and forced myself upright, every movement dragging against pain that refused to end.

Draven laughed—a low, menacing sound that made the air itself shiver. "Ah, there he is. My favorite warrior. Still standing."

"Shut. Up," I rasped, chest heaving.

His eyes gleamed like shards of glass as he stepped closer, savoring my pain. "You still cling to that pathetic spark of defiance. It is almost endearing." He tilted his head, lips curling into a cruel smile. "Do not worry, Leaf. Soon, that will burn out too. And when Strong Haven falls, you will be the one who brings it to its knees."

Reaching for my dagger, I whipped it free and raised it high, ready to drive it straight through Draven's heart—but my body refused. My arm froze midair, every muscle locked in place. Panic flared as invisible chains coiled through my limbs, pinning me where I stood. I strained, willing myself to move, to fight, to *do anything*—but I was helpless.

Draven's cloak snapped open like the wings of some great shadow, and in an instant, he was upon me. His hand closed around my wrist, prying the dagger from my grip. The blade flew from his hand and buried itself in a tree with a dull *thunk*.

"Such spirit," he murmured, his voice swirled with mock affection. His long, cold fingers clamped around my throat, lifting me effortlessly from the ground. His grip tightened, stealing what little breath I had left, black spots flooding my vision.

"Give me the stone."

The vibration in his words crawled under my skin, tugging at my will, twisting my resolve until my hand moved of its own accord. My fingers slipped into my pocket, trembling, and pulled out the aquoise. I tried to hold on—to resist—but it was useless. I handed it to him.

Draven licked his lips, eyes gleaming with cruel satisfaction. Then he let go, and I dropped to the dirt, gasping.

"Thank you, Leaf," he said, voice rich with mockery. "And thank you for trying to kill me in the dungeon. Without you, I would not be standing here, holding this precious stone."

I wiped the blood from my mouth, staring up at him through the blur of pain. "What will you do now?"

A menacing smile spread across his face as he held the stone between his thumb and forefinger, lifting it toward the light. Such a small thing—fragile, beautiful—and yet it held immense power. My stomach twisted. I could only imagine how he meant to use it.

"Well," Draven said softly, admiring the stone as

though it were a crown jewel, "now I will take control of Faevenly."

The words struck like a death knell, echoing through the stillness. I wanted to lunge for him, to end him, to take back what I had stolen—but my body refused, bound by his will. All I could do was watch as he turned, cloak whispering against the earth, the stone's light casting blue across the shadows.

This was not over. Not even close. And in that moment, as darkness swallowed him whole, I swore I would break free —no matter what it took.

The air hung heavier after he left, like something in the world had shifted—like the balance had tipped in his favor. The power he now held, it wasn't just a threat to me. It was bigger than that. Far bigger.

I was not only fighting for my life anymore. I was fighting for Gabriela.

And he was coming for her next.

CONCLUSION OF BOOK THREE

Everything has changed.
And there's no turning back.

Continue the story in *Fae Rising*.
The fate of Faevenly hangs in the balance.

Start Book 4 now.

THE FAE BLOODLINES SERIES

Fae Away, book 1

Fae Fractured, book 2

Fae Hunted, book 3

Fae Rising, book 4

For a full listing of Rose's books, visit her website at
www.RoseGarciaBooks.com/GARCIAVERSE

Fae Bloodlines Series

 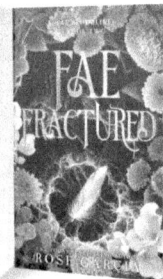  

A ROYAL ROMANTIC FANTASY SERIES
FEATURING HISPANIC CHARACTERS,
POWERFUL FAMILIES, DYNAMIC
FRIENDSHIPS, AND FORBIDDEN
ROMANCE

WWW.ROSEGARCIABOOKS.COM

ACKNOWLEDGMENTS

My love for all things fae continues!

When I finished Fae Away and Fae Fractured, I knew I wanted to keep going with the Fae Bloodlines series. But who would I write about? And what would be their story?

At first, I toyed with the idea of doing something with a young Celyse and Julio, but for some reason that idea never really grabbed me. I thought they'd been through enough and so I wanted them to have a good long run at a happy life in the human realm.

But then, an idea struck me. What if I did something with the next generation? That's when I started asking myself all the "what if' questions. What if Julio and Celyse had a daughter with the signature Avila witchy powers? What if Draven somehow escaped from his magical sleep in the dungeon? What if he still wanted revenge? Because, you know, of course he'd want revenge!

These ideas really excited me!

Hence, Gabriela was born. And since I had already introduced a young Leaf in Fae Fractured who had an antagonist relationship with Julio, I knew he'd be perfect as the love interest.

And the villain? Good ole crystal-eyed Draven was primed for revenge. He is so wicked!

And that's how Fae Hunted came to be and I love this story so much! I hope you did too!

Now, on to the acknowledgements!

First and foremost, my faith is an important part of my life, so I most definitely give thanks to God for keeping me and my family safe and healthy.

I am so very thankful for my family for always supporting and encouraging me. And a huge shoutout to my writer besties, the Queens of the Quill.

I am beyond grateful for my reader group, The Rose Bud Society, and all the readers who have found my books and loved my stories and have come to my signings and events. Y'ALL COMPLETE ME!

I could go on and on with thanking people, so let me just say, for those who've cheered me on and supported me, thank you, thank you, thank you! I am so very grateful!

ABOUT THE AUTHOR

Rose Garcia is a USA Today bestselling author and screenwriter known for crafting heart-stopping fantasy stories where belief is power, love defies all, and hope burns brightest. Magic is real in her world—and the only thing more dangerous than a broken heart... is a hopeful one.

A lawyer turned writer, Rose weaves stories of complicated romance, powerful families, deep-rooted friendships, and ancestral magic drawn from her Mexican American heritage. Her diverse heroes are driven by bold hearts, forced to confront tangled destinies and make impossible choices.

When she's not writing, you can find her designing escape rooms for her husband, obsessing over fantasy shows, traveling, or hanging out with her needy and precious rescue dogs.

Rose lives in Houston, Texas, and believes tacos are a core food group—because well, they are.

For more on Rose, visit www.rosegarciabooks.com.

Join Rose's FB Group!
www.facebook.com/groups/TheRoseBudSociety
Subscribe to Rose's newsletter!
www.rosegarciabooks.com/newsletter

A final request: please review her books and spread the word about her stories! She would be most appreciative.